Nancy Drew®
in
The Whispering Statue

This Armada book belongs to:

_____

_____

_____

The Nancy Drew Mystery Stories®

The Whispering Statue

Carolyn Keene

Armada

First published in the U.K. by
William Collins Sons & Co. Ltd., London and Glasgow.
First published in Armada in 1977 by
Fontana Paperbacks,
8 Grafton Street, London W1X 3LA.

This impression 1984.

Printed in Great Britain by
William Collins Sons & Co. Ltd., Glasgow.

CONTENTS

The old man threw up his arms in alarm

·1· *Togo's Prank*

NANCY DREW, her hands thrust deeply in her sweater pockets, paused in front of the Marvin residence. She gave a soft call. Almost at once the door flew open and two girls came outside. One was Bess Marvin, the other a girl cousin of Bess named George Fayne.

"Am I late?" Nancy inquired as her chums joined her. "I hurried as fast as I could but everything seemed to delay me."

"Oh, we'll be in plenty of time for the opening ceremonies at the park," Bess replied carelessly. "The programme isn't scheduled to start until two o'clock."

"I'd just as soon miss the speeches anyway," George laughed, falling into step with her companions. "I'm mostly interested in seeing the grand new park."

The three girls, who lived in River Heights, were walking towards Harrison Park, to attend the formal opening exercises. The property itself, comprising many acres, was located on the outskirts of the city along the banks of a small lake. It had been willed to River Heights by the late Mary Harrison, a wealthy old lady who had set aside ample funds to maintain the grounds as a place of beauty and recreation.

"It will be the very nicest park in the city," Bess remarked enthusiastically as she walked swiftly on.

"I hear too, that part of the lake is to be cemented off for a swimming pool."

As they approached the arched entrance gate, the girls heard band music and hastened their steps. It was Saturday afternoon, and the streets were crowded with cars while the walks were thronged with men, women and children in a gay holiday mood.

"Oh, isn't that garden gorgeous?" Bess murmured a moment later, catching a glimpse of red, lavender and yellow flowers directly ahead.

Neither Nancy nor George replied, for they had heard a soft pad-pad behind them, and had turned to see who was following so closely at their heels.

"Why, it's a little dog!" Nancy exclaimed in delight. "Isn't he cute?"

She did not need to coax the bull-terrier to come closer, for he trotted up to be petted. As the Drew girl stooped to pat his well-shaped head he leaped at her in friendly fashion and pawed her dress.

"What is your name, doggie?" she asked, pushing him from her. "And where is your collar?"

"Evidently he has run away," George declared. "Of course he's not a stray. You can tell he's a thorough-bred."

"Yes, he looks like a valuable dog," Nancy agreed, glancing round the park in search of the animal's owner. "But he seems to be lost."

"Oh, come along, girls," Bess urged impatiently. "Time's going and there's so much to see."

"I suppose the dog's master is somewhere in the park," Nancy remarked, as the three friends walked on again. She glanced over her shoulder. "Why, the little scamp is following us."

"He seems to have adopted you, Nancy," George chuckled. "I hope he doesn't trail us all round the park."

Nancy halted and sternly ordered the dog to go home. He retreated a few feet and the girls continued on their way again. A moment later the terrier was trotting along beside them. Nancy tried once more to send him away, but was unsuccessful.

"You don't say 'go home' as if you really mean it, Nancy," George criticised her chum. "I'll show you how to get rid of the little scamp."

She picked up a small stick and lightly touched the dog. He regarded her reproachfully but would not retreat.

"Oh, let him follow us if he likes," Nancy urged. "He's such a friendly little fellow, and we may run into his master somewhere in the park."

"I wish we knew his name," Bess remarked. "We might call him Togo."

Togo trotted along contentedly at Nancy's heels, and presently the girls forgot about him as they paused to admire a fountain. Suddenly they were startled to hear a man shout angrily:

"Say, get your dog out of that flower-bed!"

In horror, the girls whirled round to see Togo digging furiously for a bone he thought was there. Plants and dirt were flying in every direction.

Nancy and her chums called sternly to the dog but he paid no heed. Finally George caught the mischievous little fellow in her arms and yanked him out of the bed. He had made several ugly holes in the soft earth. Broken flowers were scattered over the grass.

"You have no right to bring a dog into a park unless

you keep him on a leash," said a bystander to the girls. "The flower bed is now practically ruined."

"He's not our dog," George replied, flushing deeply.

She put the squirming Togo down on the ground. As the three girls scurried away, conscious that many persons were regarding them with disapproval, the terrier followed them again.

"Oh, what shall we do with the dog?" Bess moaned under her breath. "Everyone thinks he's our pet."

"A park policeman will be after us if we're not careful," Nancy said uneasily. "Please go home, Togo; or if you don't know where 'home' is, go somewhere."

The terrier stared at her almost impishly. After a while he moved away, and the girls hoped that he would leave them. The next instant they were dismayed to see him dart towards the lake where three swans were gliding serenely along close to shore. Barking excitedly, Togo ran along the bank, making little dives at the frightened birds.

"Oh, capture him before he swims in," Bess wailed. "That dog will cause our arrest before he gets finished!"

Nancy and George cornered the animal, pulling him forcibly away from shore. They scolded him severely, but their words were only wasted. The mischievous terrier barked, frightened children by darting towards them, and cast a wistful eye at every flower-bed they passed.

Soon the girls felt that everyone in their vicinity was regarding them with disapproval. Over and over, they explained that Togo was not their dog; but with the little fellow following so worshipfully at their heels they could not expect to be believed. Several times Nancy and her chums tried to sneak away, but the alert Togo always found them again.

"Oh, let's sit down on this bench and try to keep the scamp out of mischief for a minute or two," Nancy sighed, indicating a seat which offered an excellent view of the lake.

"Is it safe, do you think?" Bess murmured. "The swans may come sailing along."

"Oh, I'll keep my hands on Togo every second," Nancy declared. "If this dog were mine I'd get a good strong leash for him."

"He may be your dog if the owner isn't found," George chuckled. "I can see where your work is cut out for you."

"Oh, no," Nancy corrected quickly, "if the owner doesn't show up he's your dog, George. You saw him first."

"We'll let Togo decide for himself," George laughed. "Of course he'll choose you."

Presently two women sat down on a bench near by. Nancy promptly tightened her hold upon Togo, for she could not tell what he might try to do. The newcomers were well dressed, and from their appearance and general conversation, Nancy gathered that the older of the two might be one of the speakers on the dedication programme.

"I am dreadfully nervous," the silver-haired lady confessed to her companion. "You see, this is the first time I have ever addressed such a large audience, and the first time that I have faced a microphone. I'm so afraid I'll forget my speech."

"Oh, nonsense, Mrs Owen," the other replied encouragingly. "If you weren't a capable speaker, the Federation of Women's Clubs never would have selected you as their representative here today."

"Oh, it is a high honour, and that's why I am so uneasy. I have had no radio experience. If you don't mind, I think I'll just run through my notes again."

The woman addressed as Mrs Owen opened her handbag. She removed several folded papers and scanned them intently.

"I've heard my mother mention Mrs Owen," Bess whispered to her chums. "She's a very prominent clubwoman who has made dozens of speeches around River Heights. I can't imagine her being nervous."

After scanning her notes for several minutes, Mrs Owen glanced at her watch and rose.

"I am scheduled to give my talk in exactly thirty minutes so I think we may as well go to the stands right away."

The women walked along slowly. Not until they had disappeared from view did Nancy notice that Mrs Owen had left her handbag lying on the park bench.

"Oh, the poor woman will be terribly upset when she discovers her loss!" she cried. "We must give the handbag to her before she makes her speech."

The girls moved forward to pick up the bag. Before they could do so, Togo, who seemed to guess their intention, darted ahead of them directly for the bench.

"Togo!" Nancy called sharply, but she was unable to distract the dog.

He leaped upon the vacant seat, and to the horror of the girls, picked up Mrs Owen's handbag in his mouth.

"Bring it here!" Nancy commanded firmly.

Instead, Togo jumped down, and with the bag still in his jaws, he trotted playfully in the opposite direction.

"Oh, he's going towards the lake!" Bess cried in alarm.

"Togo!" George screamed, starting to run after the terrier.

It was exactly the wrong thing to do, for Togo, thinking that the girl wished to frolic with him, leaped faster and faster to the very edge of the lake. There he hesitated only an instant before plunging in. With the handbag still grasped in his mouth he swam away, head held proudly out of the water.

"Oh, what shall we do now?" Bess moaned.

As she had feared, Togo, after swimming out a short distance, had dropped the bag. The mischief accomplished, he then swam back to shore. Shaking the water from his sleek coat, he looked at Nancy as if expecting praise.

"Mrs Owen's speech in the bottom of the lake!" George exclaimed in dismay. "Now what will she do?"

"Let's get away from this park before anything more happens," Bess shuddered. "Let's go home."

Nancy shook her head. "We must find Mrs Owen and try to explain. There's just a chance that the bag can be brought up."

"Not in time for her speech," Bess replied gloomily. "The water is too deep for wading, even if we should want to ruin our clothing. There's nothing we can do."

Nancy held a different opinion. She had marked the exact spot where the bag had dropped in the water, and she believed that if she could only find the park workmen in time, they might drag the lake and retrieve the bag within a few minutes.

"Wait here," she commanded her chums. "Don't take your eyes from the spot where Togo dropped the bag. I'll be right back."

Nancy darted away, hurrying directly to the speakers'

stand where Mrs Owen was engaged in excited conversation with several of the officials.

"Oh, I don't know what to do," the woman was saying nervously. "I've just discovered my bag is missing and all my notes are in it. I can't make a speech without them."

"Oh, but you must, Mrs Owen," one of the men urged. "We are depending upon you to make the dedication. No one else is prepared."

"It's not merely the speech," the woman continued in distress. "The bag also contained considerable money and a gift which I was asked to present today. It is from the Federation of Women's Clubs."

"We'll do the best we can," an official returned grimly, "but I'm afraid we'll not recover your bag before the ceremonies start—if we recover it at all."

Nancy had reached the platform in time to hear the last remark. She pushed through the group of men and reached Mrs Owen's side.

"I can tell you what became of your bag!" she cried.

"Oh, where is it? Where is my bag?"

Briefly, Nancy revealed the prank played by the mischievous Togo. The woman sagged into the nearest chair.

"Then my notes—the gift—everything is gone."

"I saw exactly where the handbag went down," Nancy said eagerly. "If the park workmen will help, I think we can recover it in time."

"In twenty minutes?" Mrs Owen gasped, glancing at her watch. "Oh, it isn't possible!"

"Yes, it is," Nancy insisted firmly, "but there's not a second to waste! We must act!"

·2· *A Strange Resemblance*

MRS OWEN was too excited and nervous to have any definite idea about what could be done to recover the lost handbag. She dared not leave the stand to aid in the search, for in a very few minutes it would be time for her to speak. How much of her speech she could remember without notes, she could not guess.

It was Nancy who hastened to find park workmen. She pushed her way through the crowds, closely followed by several officials.

"There's not a chance we can find the handbag before the ceremonies begin," one of the men murmured. "It would be useless to try."

Nancy did not bother to answer. Instead, she darted into a nearby building obviously used for housing park equipment. Fortune favoured her, for she found two men inside who were cleaning their tools. Tersely she told them about the lost bag, earnestly requesting that they help her recover it from the lake.

"Not much chance of getting it, I'm afraid," one of the workmen responded as he went on scraping dirt from a spade. "It would take half a day to drag the lake, and even then the bag might not be found."

"But I know *exactly* where it went down," Nancy insisted, becoming just slightly excited. "You don't understand—it's very important that I recover the handbag now."

Then, although valuable time was being consumed, she explained that the bag contained not only Mrs Owen's notes but also a gift.

"If you noticed just where the bag fell, we might get it out," the older of the two workmen said, his attitude undergoing a sudden change. "But I doubt if it can be done before the ceremony starts."

"Oh, we must have it before then," Nancy murmured. "Please try."

"We'll do the best we can."

The men then moved with alacrity, hauling out equipment which had been used the previous day to dredge leaves and debris from the lake bed. While they were loading it into a rowboat at the water's edge, Nancy hastened on ahead to the place where George and Bess were waiting. True to their friend's command, they had kept their eyes glued upon the spot where Togo had dropped the handbag.

"I believe we'll salvage the bag after all," Nancy told her chums triumphantly. "Workmen are coming with a boat. Oh, why are they so slow?"

Anxiously she glanced up the shore and then peered nervously at her wrist watch. How swiftly the minutes were slipping away, and every second was precious.

As a band stationed near the stands started to play, George gasped in dismay, "The ceremonies are beginning!"

Nancy nodded soberly. "If the workmen don't find the bag in time and Mrs Owen fails in her speech, I'll feel that it is my fault."

It was typical of Nancy Drew to blame herself,

although many times no other person would think of considering her responsible. Certainly, she could not be charged with Togo's wild prank. Ever conscientious and sympathetic, Nancy enjoyed lending a helping hand to anyone in trouble. This admirable trait frequently brought difficulties upon herself, and many an adventure had resulted from her desire to aid strangers.

The girl had come quite naturally by her love of adventure, for she was the daughter of Carson Drew, a well known criminal lawyer who had won state-wide renown through his ability to solve baffling mysteries.

After her first thrilling plunge into the fascinating field of mystery and intrigue, one adventure followed another in rapid succession. As Hannah Gruen, the family housekeeper, often remarked, "Nancy just couldn't be held down." Even Carson Drew sometimes feared that his only daughter's love for adventure might some day lead her into serious trouble.

Although courageous, the girl never was recklessly so, for, left motherless at an early age, she had developed amazing judgment. This quality was recognized and respected by the girl's many friends and classmates at River Heights. Bess and George, who lived in the same neighbourhood, were proud of their chum, and liked to say that they had shared in some of her exciting experiences.

"When you're with Nancy, interesting things always seem to happen," George frequently declared. Now, as she and Bess waited for the park workmen to come with their boat, they felt like voicing the sentiment again.

"Oh, they're here at last!" Nancy cried in relief as she glimpsed the approaching craft.

From the bank of the lake she gave directions,

indicating exactly where the men were to drag for the lost handbag. Nancy and her chums were so occupied that not until a fairly large crowd had gathered did they realize that their activities were attracting attention.

"What has happened?" a woman asked Nancy, plucking at her sleeve. "Has someone gone down in the lake?"

The girl shook her head, for she had no time to answer questions. Other persons gathered along the shore, and soon many of them were saying that a child had been drowned.

"No, no, we're trying to recover a handbag," Bess corrected, but only a few persons were close enough to hear her.

As the search went on, the crowd grew in size until the girls feared that someone would be pushed into the water. Time after time, they requested persons to move back, but always those behind surged forward again.

Nancy felt someone touch her arm. Turning a trifle impatiently, she saw a tried and true friend, Ned Nickerson, who looked worried.

"Anything wrong?" he asked. "Need help?"

"Oh, Ned, try to restrain these people," said Nancy. "Tell them no one has been drowned."

Ned did not annoy the girls with any useless questions. He ordered the crowd to move back, and his voice had a ring of authority which caused people to obey. Just then a policeman came hurrying up to aid the young man.

"Oh, they've found it!" Nancy cried suddenly, as one of the boatmen held an object aloft. "The bag has been brought up!"

The water-soaked bag was placed in her hands.

"Oh, thank you for all your trouble," the Drew girl murmured gratefully. With a quick glance at her wrist watch she pushed through the crowd, then started to run towards the stands where Mrs Owen was awaiting her.

Bess and George explained the need of haste to Ned, and the three followed their friend at a more dignified pace. They quickly lost sight of her in the throng which milled near the stands, but knew that they would find her later.

Unmindful of an arrogant usher who tried to block her path, Nancy slipped past him directly up to the speakers' stand where Mrs Owen was sitting. The woman's face brightened as she observed the girl's approach. Without disturbing any of the officials who were in the box, Mrs Owen joined Nancy directly behind the wooden structure where they were out of sight from the audience.

"Oh, you wonderful girl! You recovered my notes, my money, and my gift!"

Eagerly Mrs Owen took the bag, but as she removed the water-soaked papers a look of horror returned to her face. The writing had been partially washed away, and the papers threatened to tear at the touch of a finger.

"Oh, I'm afraid they're ruined after all," the club-woman murmured. "What shall I do? I can't take these dripping papers into the speakers' box, and I must have them."

For a moment Nancy feared all her haste had been in vain. Then, recalling that she had glimpsed an electric heater at a food stand near by, it occurred to her that it might be possible to dry out the papers.

"How much time will there be before you speak?" she questioned tersely.

"Only five minutes." Mrs Owen glanced at the

speakers' box. "But that politician talking now may run on for a while."

"He sounds as if he would," Nancy nodded with a smile. "I think we'll have time to dry these papers across the way."

The attendant at the stand was only too glad to give Mrs Owen and Nancy the use of the electric heater. Quickly they emptied the handbag, spreading out all the notes and other papers.

Nancy could not fail to notice that one of the items was a neatly clipped "personal" taken from a newspaper. Before it occurred to her that such an act might be prying, she had read the brief advertisement.

"Rexy, come home. All is forgiven. Alice."

Nancy frequently had seen similar items in papers, but she wondered why a woman of Mrs Owen's type should be interested in such a clipping. Had the woman herself inserted the appeal, or did it concern some friend of hers?

The Drew girl knew that it was none of her affair. She had no time even to consider the matter, for the papers were nearly dry. Mrs Owen hastily gathered them up, taking care to replace the "personal" item in her pocket.

"Oh, dear, everything has upset me so, I'm certain I shall make a dismal failure of this talk," she murmured nervously. "I can't read half of what I've written."

"Perhaps I can help you," Nancy suggested kindly. "Try saying your speech over to me while I look at the notes. I'll prompt you."

Mrs Owen was able to give most of the talk without hesitation, and faltered at only a few places. Nancy listened intently, nodded encouragingly, and at the close, thrust the notes back into the clubwoman's trembling hand.

"Just splendid, Mrs Owen. I'm sure you'll have no trouble. And now you should hurry back, for the politician is just finishing."

"I can't thank you enough for all you've done," Mrs Owen murmured as she turned away. "I'll see you after the ceremonies—if I haven't collapsed by that time."

Not without misgivings, Nancy watched the woman make her way to the platform. The girl looked about for a place to sit. Every seat was occupied, but she was able to station herself by a pillar barely a dozen feet from the speakers' box.

Scarcely had she taken her post when Mrs Owen was introduced. Outwardly the woman appeared composed, but Nancy could tell that she was still nervous.

The speaker began well, consulting her notes only at infrequent intervals. Nancy relaxed somewhat, and then, just as she felt that all would be smooth sailing, the woman faltered. She peered down at the words before her, seemingly unable to read them.

Like a flash the words which should come next entered Nancy's mind. She whispered them just loud enough for Mrs Owen to hear. The woman understood, and taking heart, went on with her speech. Once towards the end she nearly broke down, but was aided by Nancy's timely prompting. Finally she presented the gift, and as she finished, was greeted by a generous amount of handclapping.

Since Nancy had no seat, she soon grew tired of standing by the stone pillar, and moved away. As she was wandering towards one of the refreshment stands, she was joined by Ned and her chums who had sighted her from afar.

"Mrs Owen didn't do half badly," Bess laughed. "I thought for a minute that she couldn't read her notes, and my heart leaped right up in my throat."

"So did mine," Nancy confessed with a chuckle. She did not detract from Mrs Owen's speech by revealing how she had aided her.

"I've had enough of speeches," Ned broke into the conversation. "Let's go over to the casino and have some ice cream."

The girls quickly accepted the invitation, and presently all were enjoying refreshments in the modern amusement building. Afterwards the young people indulged in a few of the games, and Nancy was delighted when her bowling score won a prize.

"A box of stationery," Bess observed as the package was unwrapped.

"I don't know what I'll do with it," Nancy replied. "I seldom have time to write letters any more."

"Oh, you'll have plenty of leisure time during your vacation," George responded carelessly.

"Vacation?" Ned inquired quickly. "Are you going away, Nancy?"

"Only for a few weeks, Ned. Dad has some business to transact at Sea Cliff, so he said I could go along and take Bess and George with me."

"Sea Cliff?" Ned repeated thoughtfully. "That's on the Atlantic Coast, isn't it? I wish I could get there myself."

Before the girls could make a response, Mrs Owen came hastening towards them. The dedication exercises had ended some minutes earlier and the crowd was dispersing.

"Oh, here you are," the clubwoman cried, addressing Nancy. "I searched everywhere for you. I want to tell you how wonderful you were to help me through my speech, and I'd like to know your name."

"Nancy Drew."

"Why, I've heard of you," Mrs Owen replied in astonishment. "Of course, I know your father by reputation. I should have failed completely today if you hadn't prompted me."

"I was afraid you might not be able to hear me whisper."

"Oh, I did, very distinctly, yet I am confident the audience didn't catch on. Miss Drew, as you sat crouched there by the stone pillar, your pose was most arresting."

"My pose?" Nancy asked, slightly bewildered.

"Yes, even in my frantic state of mind I noticed it instantly. You reminded me of a marble statue I once saw which was called 'The Whispering Girl.' Tell me, did you ever do any modelling for a sculptor?"

"Oh, no," Nancy answered, somewhat embarrassed because she saw that Ned and her chums were deeply impressed by the comparison Mrs Owen had made. "Where is this statue, may I ask?"

The clubwoman's response was a surprising one.

"It is located at a place called Old Estate. I saw it years ago when I was visiting in Sea Cliff."

·3· *The Whispering Girl*

"Did I understand you to say Sea Cliff?" Nancy inquired in astonishment.

"Yes," Mrs Owen replied. "It is a summer resort place along the Atlantic Coast. Old Estate is located on the shore and was falling into ruin when last I saw it. By this time the house and the statue as well may have been washed into the sea."

"Oh, I hope not," Nancy said quickly, "because I'd like very much to see it. My chums and I are leaving in a few days to spend a vacation at Sea Cliff."

"Then by all means you must visit Old Estate to view yourself in marble," Mrs Owen smiled. "Your resemblance to the statue is really amazing, Miss Drew."

"I certainly shall see it," Nancy declared, and then asked the clubwoman how to reach Old Estate after arriving at Sea Cliff.

The girl wrote down the directions on the back of an old envelope. Upon Mrs Owen's request she gave her own address in River Heights. The clubwoman was noting it in her little book when Bess suddenly gave an exclamation of dismay.

"Oh, look who's here!"

"Togo!" George cried with a laugh. "He has followed Nancy to the casino."

The girls had congratulated themselves that they were free of the mischievous little dog, for after dropping Mrs Owen's handbag in the lake he had lost himself somewhere in the crowd. Now Togo stood in the entrance of the casino, looking alertly round him.

"Let's hope he doesn't see us," Nancy murmured.

Even as she spoke, the terrier gave a joyful bark and bounded towards the young people. He darted directly in front of a dignified waiter with a heavy tray, and struck the man full force just below the knees. The waiter stumbled wildly in an effort to maintain his balance, then fell backwards against the wall. His tray of dishes crashed to the floor.

"Oh, what will Togo do next?" Bess wailed. "Let's get away from here before we're accused of being his owner."

Escape, however, was out of the question, for the little dog, oblivious of the havoc he had wrought, came up to Nancy and leaped against her. Nearly everyone in the room turned to stare at the young people, much to their confusion. The manager of the place came towards the party angrily.

"Dogs are *not* allowed in this casino," he said in freezing tones, addressing the embarrassed Nancy.

"He isn't my dog, even if he does follow me round everywhere," she replied humbly.

"Just get the animal out of here, that's all I ask," the manager answered grimly. He made a dive for Togo, who by this time had lost interest in Nancy and playfully was attacking another waiter.

"I'll try," Nancy murmured contritely. "Come here, Togo!" she ordered.

The little animal came obediently to her side. She

picked him up in her arms, and the party hastily left the casino.

"So this was the little dog that took my handbag," Mrs Owen laughed, giving the terrier a friendly pat. "He does manage to keep busy, doesn't he?"

Nancy dropped the dog to the ground, and Ned chased him away to another section of the park. When the young man returned alone, Mrs Owen was saying good-bye to Nancy and her chums.

"I'm in favour of going home myself before Togo picks up my trail again," laughed Nancy.

Ned had his car at the park and offered to drive the girls, but they declined, preferring to walk. At the Fayne residence, Nancy took leave of George. A few minutes later she was saying good-bye to Bess, when the latter gave a little squeal of consternation.

"Oh, Nancy, here he comes again!"

The girl turned to see Togo trotting down the sidewalk towards them.

"The little pest!" she exclaimed. "What are we to do with him?"

"What are *you* to do, you mean?" Bess corrected with a wicked chuckle. "He's your dog, not mine."

She ran into the house and from the window, watched in amusement as Togo joyfully greeted his chosen mistress. With a sigh Nancy continued down the street, the terrier following close at her heels. Reaching home, she slipped inside, leaving the dog on the porch. Half an hour later he was still there.

"Oh, I'll just have to weaken," she decided, opening the door and allowing the pet to come in. "He's homeless and perhaps hungry."

Mrs Gruen, the housekeeper who had worked at the

Drew residence for so many years that she was regarded almost as a member of the family, came into the living room, halting abruptly when she saw the dog.

"Nancy Drew, where on earth did you find that dirty little animal? You know I can't have him here muddying up the rugs."

"I'll give Togo a bath," promised Nancy. "I think he'll be fairly presentable then."

"Surely you're not thinking of *keeping* him?"

"I don't seem to have any choice in the matter," Nancy laughed. "He followed me all afternoon at the park. Poor little fellow! I imagine he's had nothing to eat for days."

She had made a direct appeal to the housekeeper's sympathies, and as she hoped, Mrs Gruen grudgingly went to the kitchen to find food for Togo. She softened somewhat, as Nancy told her about the terrier's antics.

"He seems to be a smart little dog," Mrs Gruen admitted, "but if he's mischievous I can't have him around."

"Oh, I imagine it was only because he was so hungry," Nancy answered hastily. "He'll probably be very good from now on."

"He'll eat as much as a grown person does."

"You can give him some of my portion," Nancy smiled. "You see, since Togo followed me home I really feel it is my duty to keep him until his master is found."

"Your duty!" Mrs Gruen laughed. "That's only an excuse you thought up. You really like the scamp, and hope his owner never does claim him again."

The front door opened to admit Carson Drew. The lawyer dropped his briefcase carelessly on a chair. Before he could greet Nancy or the housekeeper Togo had leaped up on him and tried to lick his hand.

"Well, well, where did *you* come from?" Mr Drew laughed.

The voice of the lawyer seemed to excite the terrier even more. He ran madly about the room. Before Nancy could capture him, he had snatched the leather briefcase from the chair. The flap fell open and papers scattered over the room.

"Just a nice little dog," Mrs Gruen remarked with a tinge of sarcasm.

"Togo is a bit impulsive," Nancy admitted, taking the briefcase away from him and picking up the scattered papers. "Why Dad, what's this?"

She indicated an envelope which bore the title "Charles Owen." The surname had drawn her attention.

"Oh, a letter from one of my clients," the lawyer answered. "It's not so important, but some of those other papers are. I don't want any of them to be lost."

Nancy carefully replaced all the documents in the briefcase. Then, after having tied Togo outdoors, she told her father of her adventure that afternoon at the park.

"Mrs Owen was very pleasant, Dad," she remarked, "but I couldn't help thinking——"

"That she has a mysterious background?" Mr Drew finished teasingly.

"I shouldn't have used exactly that expression," Nancy smiled. "But you must admit it seems odd that she'd carry a "personal" item in her bag. When I noticed that your client's name was Charles Owen it occurred to me that they might be related."

"Oh, I doubt it, Nancy. Owen is a fairly common name, you know. Mr Owen is connected with the firm

Owen and Wormrath, located along the Atlantic Coast. They have a small branch office in this state too."

"I suppose my idea is fantastic," Nancy admitted. "Even if Mrs Owen were related it probably would mean nothing."

The girl promptly dismissed the matter from her mind and forgot about the clubwoman entirely until a few days later, when a messenger delivered a large box of candy sent to her by Mrs Owen as a token of her appreciation. Nancy wrote a note of thanks.

The week slipped away so swiftly that almost before the girls realized it, they were boarding the train with Mr Drew, bound for Sea Cliff and a happy vacation.

"I'll miss Togo," Nancy remarked to George and Bess as they all waited on the station platform. "Mrs Gruen didn't like the idea of watching out for him while Dad and I are away, but of course we couldn't take him along."

"He'd probably leave a trail of wreckage behind him," George chuckled.

"Togo isn't as bad as he was," Nancy said proudly. "I've been trying to train him."

"Trying is right," Mr Drew cut in. "You'll never conquer Togo, Nancy, so you may as well admit defeat at the start."

The block signal had dropped, and a few minutes later the flyer came roaring into the station. Mr Drew's party was hustled aboard by the conductor.

"This your dog?" the trainman demanded gruffly.

Nancy glanced back in surprise and collapsed weakly against her father's arm. Togo, who evidently had broken his leash, followed the party to the station, and leaped aboard the train just as it pulled out.

"You can't have the dog in here," the conductor said sternly. "He must go into the baggage car."

Togo had very definite ideas of his own. Before either the conductor or Mr Drew could capture him, he had scampered down the aisle. Deciding that he would like to sit beside an old lady in a flowing black cape who occupied a seat towards the front of the car, he leaped up alongside of her.

The woman dropped the book she was reading and gave a startled cry. She tried to push Togo away. The dog, thinking it was all in play, began to tear at her cloak, entangling himself in its generous folds.

"Togo!" Nancy Drew cried furiously. She caught the dog but his teeth held fast to the cape. As the garment billowed outwards, the girl noticed an astonishing thing.

The inside of the cape contained several pockets heavily weighted down as if with money!

The elderly woman jerked her cloak together, frowning severely at Nancy.

"I'm so sorry," the girl apologized. "I hope Togo didn't bite you."

"No," answered the woman shortly, "but please take him away."

Nancy was only too glad to retreat with Togo held firmly under her arm. As she walked down the aisle she was the target of all eyes. However, she was scarcely aware of it, for her own attention had been drawn to a dark-haired young man who occupied the seat directly opposite the woman in the cape. He was a sharp, shrewd looking individual, and Nancy was a little afraid that he too had seen the money which the old lady carried upon her person.

She had no time just then to worry about it, for the

conductor showed signs of making a great deal of trouble about Togo. Mr Drew finally arranged for the dog to be taken to the baggage car.

When the party was comfortably settled, Nancy told her chums about the hidden money which she had observed under the old lady's cloak, adding that she was afraid the man directly across the aisle had seen it too.

"He looks like a sharper," George observed, turning to stare at the person under discussion. "His smile is innocent enough but he has wicked eyes."

"Why, he's trying to attract that old lady's attention already," Bess added in alarm.

"Just what I feared he would do," Nancy declared, nodding. "He'll manage to get into conversation with her, and the first thing we know, her money will be gone."

As the young people watched, the man moved over into the seat across the aisle and bowed politely to its occupant. Soon he was chatting pleasantly with the old lady, but as he talked his eyes roved frequently to the cape.

"He *is* interested in her money," Nancy murmured anxiously. "Oh, dear, if he steals it I'll feel responsible."

When the conductor came through the car a few minutes later she asked him if he knew either of the passengers.

"The old lady is Miss Morse from Sea Cliff," the trainman responded. "I have never seen the man before."

Nancy felt that it was her duty to warn Miss Morse to be on her guard, yet obviously she could not talk with her until the young man should go back to his own seat. Then it might be too late. Mr Drew had gone to the observation car so she could not seek his advice.

"I'm going to take that section directly behind the couple and hear what they are saying," she indicated to her chums. "We may have misjudged the man."

She walked up the aisle and sat in the empty seat without being noticed by the pair in front. Miss Morse was staring fixedly at the strange young man as if fascinated by his face.

"Yes, I thought from the moment I first set eyes upon you that we might be related, Mr Mitza," Nancy heard her say. "How fortunate that we chanced to meet."

"Fortunate indeed!" thought Nancy. "Mr Mitza has trumped up that story to throw her off guard."

From what she overheard, it was obvious that the unscrupulous young man deliberately was finding out from Miss Morse about her personal affairs. Satisfied that she could not help just then, Nancy returned to her chums.

An hour later Alton Junction was reached, which was the point at which passengers bound for Sea Cliff must transfer to another train. As Mr Drew and the girls left the car, Nancy observed that both Miss Morse and Mr Mitza were gathering up their luggage.

"Oh, let me help you with your heavy bag," the Drew girl said quickly to the old lady, before the young man could make a similar offer.

Joe Mitza scowled at Nancy, but she paid no attention to him, hurrying the elderly woman from the car.

"I've only a minute to talk," Nancy began in an undertone, "but I want to give you a friendly warning. I'm very much afraid Mr Mitza is interested in your money. I'd not have anything to do with him if I were you."

Miss Morse stared angrily at the girl, her lips tightening into unpleasant lines.

"I'll thank you to mind your own affairs," she said sharply. "For years I've battled the world, and I'm still capable of looking after myself!"

· 4 ·   A Warning Declined

"I DIDN'T mean to interfere," Nancy said hastily. "I merely thought—that is, in a way if you should lose your money it would be my fault because of the dog——"

She began to stammer, painfully aware of Miss Morse's increasing anger.

"Oh, now I recognize you! You're the girl with the ferocious dog!"

"Well, scarcely ferocious," Nancy smiled. "Togo is rather impulsive, but as I told you before, I'm very sorry he annoyed you. However, I'm not his owner."

Miss Morse tossed her head indignantly, obviously disbelieving Nancy. Upon seeing Joe Mitza who had alighted from the train, she waved to him. Immediately the man hurried up and with a sly, triumphant glance directed at the crestfallen Nancy, picked up Miss Morse's suitcase. The peculiar couple then walked away together.

Nancy looked about for her own party. She found her father and the girls exercising Togo, who had just been taken from the baggage car.

"Oh, cheer up," Mr Drew advised his daughter kindly when he learned of the rebuff. "You've done all you can. I imagine the old lady really is capable of taking care of her money. She appears to be rather shrewd."

While Togo was allowed to trot up and down the station platform, held firmly by a suitcase strap which had been attached to his collar, Mr Drew discussed with his daughter what should be done. Although he did not like to be annoyed with Togo at Sea Cliff, it seemed out of the question to return him to Hannah Gruen.

"I'll keep him under control somehow," Nancy promised with a laugh. "Perhaps Togo will reform and be a good dog."

While Mr Drew arranged for the transfer to another train, the girls idled about the platform with Togo. A child unexpectedly separated herself from her nurse and ran excitedly towards the dog.

"Jester! Jester!" she cried joyfully, gathering the terrier into her arms.

Nancy and her chums were nonplussed. They did not know what to make of the situation.

"He's my dog," the little girl declared, trying to take the leash from Nancy's hand. "Let me have him."

"Why certainly, if he is your pet," Nancy agreed, her heart sinking. She had not realized until now how fond she was of Togo, and that it would be hard for her to give him up.

"Jester ran away about a month ago and I've looked everywhere for him," the child went on, gazing at the girls a trifle accusingly.

Just at that moment, the nurse appeared. She frowned in perplexity as she gazed at the terrier which her young charge claimed.

"Are you certain this dog is Jester, Barbara?" she

asked doubtfully. "It looks like your pet, but you know we thought Jester had been run over by an automobile."

"This is Jester," the child insisted stubbornly. "I want him back."

"Togo doesn't seem to know you," Nancy observed. "I admit the dog is a stray, but I found him a long distance from here—at River Heights."

"You're lying because you don't want to give me my dog," the child stormed. "I know you found Jester here in Alton Junction."

"I can prove that he came from River Heights," Nancy insisted, growing irritated. "Here comes my father, and he'll confirm it."

Carson Drew listened with a sympathetic ear to the child's claim, but said kindly that he felt certain that Togo could not be the lost Jester, for River Heights was too far away for the dog to have strayed such a distance.

"My mother will make you give up the dog!" the child screamed furiously. "Mother! Mother!"

A tall, well-dressed woman, beautifully groomed, came up haughtily to confront Nancy and her friends.

"What is it, Barbara dear?" she asked.

"I've found my dog, Mother, and these mean people say I can't have him!"

"What we said—" began Mr Drew politely, but the woman cut him short.

"Give the child her dog instantly or I shall call the police and have you arrested for theft!"

"Call the police!" Mr Drew challenged, for now he would not have relinquished Togo under any circumstances. "You'll not get the terrier unless you can prove that you own him."

Nancy and her chums thought the woman was only

bluffing, but they were mistaken. She did summon an officer, and for a few minutes it appeared as if Togo must be given up, for the policeman tended to side with Mrs Hastings, a well-to-do resident of Alton Junction.

However, Carson Drew calmly took the group to the baggage car. The man in charge there testified that Togo had been brought from River Heights. Then he handed one of the officers his card.

"You're Carson Drew, the lawyer?" the man asked in surprise. Upon receiving a curt nod he added with an abrupt change of tone, "Well, well, I never thought I'd meet you, Mr Drew. I've heard about your work——"

"We're in a hurry to catch a train," the attorney interrupted. "What about the dog? Do we keep him or don't we?"

"Yes, it's obvious the little girl is mistaken. I'm sorry you were delayed, Mr Drew."

Mrs Hastings might have offered a similar apology, but with an angry toss of her head she caught Barbara by the hand and marched away.

"We lost a wonderful chance to get rid of Togo," Mr Drew chuckled as they hurried to find the Sea Cliff train. "Not sorry, are you, Nancy?"

"I want Togo to have a good master," the girl replied. "That's why I hope to keep him myself for a while."

Mr Drew and his party boarded the train only a minute before it left the station. Towards the rear of the car Nancy observed Miss Morse and Mr Mitza chatting together like old friends, but she did not show any interest in the pair. When they reached Sea Cliff she lost sight of the couple at the station.

A taxicab carried Mr Drew, the girls and Togo to one

of the leading hotels located along the ocean front. On being assigned to the room which she would share with George and Bess, Nancy's first act was to throw open the window and breathe deeply of the salty air.

"Just listen to the pounding of the waves against the rocks!" she exclaimed. "I love the ocean."

"We'll have a wonderful time here," George declared gaily. "How long do you think we can stay, Nancy?"

"It's hard to tell. It depends on how long Dad takes to attend to his business."

"I hope it requires a month," Bess laughed. "Not wishing your father any bad luck, of course."

Togo had been established in a kennel at the back of the hotel, and as soon as the girls unpacked their suitcases they went downstairs to learn how he was getting along. The terrier seemed perfectly satisfied in his new quarters and was munching upon a juicy bone which the hotel chef had given him.

The girls walked down to the beach but felt unequal to a swim. So soon after their long train ride they were content to feast their eyes upon the view.

At breakfast the next morning, Mr Drew told Nancy that he would be absent from Sea Cliff for a day or two. This was not a surprise to her for he had explained before they made the trip that business would take him away from the summer resort city.

"We'll manage to amuse ourselves while you're gone," she smiled. "Don't hurry back."

"You're not by any chance anxious to get rid of me?" the lawyer asked teasingly.

"You know better, Dad," Nancy laughed. "Togo may become mischievous again, and if so we may need you to bail us out of jail!"

After Mr Drew had gone, the girls ventured to ask the hotel clerk if he knew of a place called Old Estate in the vicinity of Sea Cliff. It was their intention to view "The Whispering Girl" statue at the first opportunity.

"I'm not sure just which place you mean," the man replied in perplexity. "There are so many ancient estates around Sea Cliff. I'll make a few inquiries and perhaps have definite information for you this afternoon."

Nancy thanked the clerk. Then another question popped into her mind.

"Oh, by the way," she asked carelessly, "do you know where Miss Morse lives?"

"Miss Morse?"

"Yes, I believe she's a rather wealthy resident of Sea Cliff."

"Her first name is Fanny, I think," Bess supplied eagerly. She had gleaned this scrap of information herself from the train conductor.

"Never heard of anyone by that name living here," the clerk returned.

He began to sort out mail, so the girls left.

"I can't understand it," Bess murmured as she sat down beside the other two on a bench overlooking the ocean. "Do you suppose our information about Miss Morse was incorrect?"

"I'd think the conductor had been mistaken," Nancy admitted, "only I heard Miss Morse tell Joe Mitza the very same thing—that she lived here in Sea Cliff."

Later the girls walked down to the business section of the little city, stopping to buy at several stores on the pretext of hearing about Miss Morse. No one knew of the woman.

"If Miss Morse is as wealthy as she appeared to be, surely she'd be known here," George commented thoughtfully.

"She was a funny type," Nancy said slowly. "It occurred to me that she might be playing a hoax upon Mitza."

"Why Nancy," Bess said in quick protest, "you thought it was the other way around at first. You were afraid Mitza might be after Miss Morse's money."

"I do sound inconsistent," Nancy admitted, laughing. "But the truth is, I've altered my opinion somewhat. I believe now that Miss Morse is a shrewd person who, to use her own words, is capable of looking after herself."

· 5 ·　The Woman of Mystery

NANCY and her chums spent the afternoon on the beach, enjoying a brisk swim and a sun bath. They talked no more of Miss Morse, assuming that she did not live in Sea Cliff after all.

As they entered their room later, the girls were astonished to find that in their absence an extra suitcase had been left inside.

"What is this?" Bess inquired, noticing it.

"All our luggage came yesterday," George added. "Is this your father's suitcase, Nancy?"

"Oh, no. Let's see the railroad tag." She stooped down to examine it. "Why girls, this belongs to Fanny Morse!"

"Well, of all things!" exclaimed Bess. "How did it get here in our room?"

"You tell me," Nancy responded dryly. "Obviously there's been some mix-up in the luggage, and the hotel people thought this bag belonged to us. That would seem to indicate that Miss Morse is registered here."

"The clerk told us he never heard of the woman," George commented.

"I know," Nancy nodded thoughtfully. "It's rather baffling, isn't it?"

She telephoned the clerk in charge who could not explain how the suitcase had been deposited in the girls' room, but assured Nancy a boy would be sent for it immediately.

The girls chose to follow the bag down to the foyer. They examined the hotel register, but Miss Morse's name had not been listed as a recent arrival. The desk man was perplexed too, for he did not know what to do with the suitcase. In vain, he questioned the bell boys. No one admitted taking the luggage to Room 305 nor did anyone remember Miss Morse by either name or by the description which Nancy furnished.

"She's certainly a woman of mystery," George sighed as they gave up the quest.

"Miss Morse must be somewhere here in Sea Cliff," Nancy declared soberly. "Possibly in the hotel. I intend to watch for her."

Deciding that Togo needed exercise, the girls took the dog for a long walk on the ocean front. They passed many fine estates, the massive houses being half hidden behind tall iron fences and a natural screen of trees and shrubs. Nancy read the name plates on several of the gates.

"I wish we could find Old Estate," she remarked. "If I go home without seeing 'The Whispering Girl' I'll be very disappointed."

Mrs Owen had provided Nancy with directions for reaching the estate, but they were too vague to be of value. Apparently the club-woman had become confused concerning the names of various streets. At any rate, the girls were unable to locate many of them. Finally they came to a pine forest dotted with several tourist camps.

"Wrong again," Nancy sighed. "Old Estate couldn't be this way."

They asked the manager of the nearest camp if he knew of the place, but the man had never heard of it. Nancy and her chums went back to the hotel feeling a trifle discouraged.

"I wish we had a car here," Nancy remarked regretfully, "then we could tour round."

Since arriving at Sea Cliff, the girls had not enjoyed themselves to any great extent. The weather had been too cold for pleasant swimming, and the resort city was not as lively as they had expected to find it. The following day when Mr Drew returned, he noticed immediately that the girls appeared downcast.

"We like it here," Nancy insisted upon being questioned, "but the most interesting things to see are miles from the city along the shore."

"Why not hire a cab and drive wherever you like?" her father questioned.

"We could do that, I suppose," Nancy said slowly, "only one always feels so rushed and money-conscious listening to the steady tick-tick, tick-tick of the taxi-meter."

Evidently Mr Drew gave some thought to the problem of transportation, for that evening when the girls joined him in the hotel dining room, they found an elderly, bent old man chatting with the lawyer. The latter arose quickly, his companion more slowly, for the poor fellow seemed to be suffering from rheumatism.

"Girls," said Mr Drew jovially, "this is Mr Harvey Trixler, the answer to your hopes. He owns an automobile and is seeking a driver."

"It's this way," Mr Trixler explained, after Nancy and her chums had seated themselves at the table. "I came to Sea Cliff to take the salt baths. For years I've suffered from rheumatism and an infection which seems to make me sore and ache in every joint. Each day I am compelled to drive out to the Brighton Baths which are ten miles from the city. Now I don't like to drive myself, and the taxi drivers seem to enjoy bumpy drives."

"As I was saying a moment ago," Mr Drew interposed with a wink at Nancy, "my daughter is an excellent driver."

"If I could help you in any way I'd be delighted to do so," Nancy offered promptly.

Before the meal ended, the girls arranged to drive the old man daily to the Brighton Baths where he usually spent the greater part of the morning. In return, they were to use the car whenever they might choose.

"Oh, Dad, how did you happen to meet Mr Trixler?" Nancy asked her father later.

"I heard him inquiring at the desk for a driver. I remembered that you girls were pining for a car of your own so I checked up on Trixler and found him to be all right, though perhaps a bit eccentric. He is a retired business man. If you can avoid jolting him too much in driving over the bumps, you'll find the arrangement a pretty good one for all concerned."

"He seems to be a rather timid sort, Dad. I'm surprised he'd be willing to trust himself to my driving."

"I told him you were very conservative," Mr Drew laughed. "I hinted that you never travel over twenty-five miles an hour."

Nancy and her chums were glad to have an occupation and really enjoyed taking Mr Trixler back and forth to the salt baths. Usually when the old man emerged from the building he would be in a gay mood, his aches and pains temporarily having been soothed away. He liked to take the girls to the cinema and frequently treated them to refreshments.

En route to the Brighton Baths it was a far different story. Then nothing seemed to please Mr Trixler. Although Nancy drove as carefully as she could he moaned at every bump and complained constantly.

Usually the old gentleman spent at least three hours inside the building. While he was occupied with the treatment the girls often drove farther along the highway, viewing the many imposing estates along the shore. Sometimes they would bring a picnic lunch and eat it either in the handsome touring car or at some rocky nook by the ocean.

During their various excursions, Nancy did not forget to inquire about Miss Morse. No one, however, seemed ever to have heard of her.

One day at noon as the girls were sitting in the car waiting for Mr Trixler, Nancy proposed that they take a walk into the pine woods directly behind the Brighton Baths.

"Too lazy," Bess yawned. "You and George go. I think I'll curl up in the back seat and snooze."

"Oh, let's stay here," George protested. "I don't seem to have any pep today either."

"I'll go myself," Nancy laughed, opening the car door. "Signal to me when Mr Trixler comes."

She walked away and turned into a trail which led through the pine woods. She had gone only a short distance when she saw that she was overtaking two men directly ahead of her. She would have thought nothing of it had she not heard the name "Miss Morse" spoken distinctly.

Instantly alert, the girl slackened her pace and gazed intently at the two men. Their backs were to her, so she could not be certain whether the younger of the two was Joe Mitza, though he resembled him.

"It *is* he!" she decided a moment later as the man turned his head slightly. "I wonder if he followed Miss Morse here?"

Nancy felt that she must learn what the two were saying. She was willing to risk detection. Pulling her hat low over her eyes, she quietly drew closer.

· 6 ·   Joe Mitza's Plot

THE two men presently sat down on a rustic bench which had been built along the trail. Nancy ducked back into the pine forest just in time to escape being seen.

As she cautiously moved forward again to approach

the bench from the rear, a stick crackled underfoot. Nancy halted, fearful that the sound might have betrayed her. She was relieved when the murmur of the men's voices went on uninterrupted.

Nancy crept near enough to hear what the two were saying. Joe Mitza was speaking.

"Oh, I marked Miss Morse as easy money the first time I set eyes on her. It was lucky for me that dog pulled open her cape. The old lady was a regular walking bank."

"How much do you figure she's good for?" the other man questioned.

"Oh, five thousand easily. Now I'll let you in on the deal, Burne, if you'll put in that amount. I'd swing it alone, only I haven't a thousand dollars to my name."

"How do I know I'll get my money back?" the man addressed as Burne asked gruffly.

"Haven't I always played square with you?" Mitza demanded sharply.

"You have so far," the other admitted, "but this old lady may not be such an easy mark as you think."

"Oh, she's stupid," Mitza replied contemptuously. "We can't go wrong on the set-up. I've already told her about a wonderful piece of ocean front property with a thriving restaurant which is supposed to cater to society people. I drove her out into the country, bought her a three dollar dinner, and showed her the Mayfair. I told her it could be bought for ten thousand, and she agreed the place would be a bargain at that."

"It would be, too," Burne observed dryly.

"You couldn't buy the Mayfair at any price," laughed Mitza, "but Miss Morse was as innocent as a babe. I gave her the good old line—that I'd never let her into the deal if I had ten thousand dollars myself. Since the Mayfair people insisted upon getting all cash I had to raise another five thousand. I suggested we buy the property in partnership."

"And she tumbled?"

"Sure. It was like taking sweets from a child. She said if I gave five thousand she'd give the other five. The money is to be sealed into an envelope and given to a third party."

"And when the envelope is opened, Miss Morse will discover that her five thousand has been replaced with fake money?"

"That's right," Mitza nodded. "The trick is an old one, but it will work on Miss Morse. You can't lose, Burne, and I'll give you a good cut on my five thousand. What do you say?"

The two men rose and walked on up the trail. Nancy waited several minutes before emerging from her hiding-place. She was aghast at the plot to steal Miss Morse's money. For just an instant, she was tempted to pursue the two swindlers and confront them with the knowledge she had gleaned, but she hesitated.

"No, I would gain nothing that way," she reflected. "Mitza would deny everything and I'd not have a scrap of evidence with which to support my claim. It will be better for me to warn Miss Morse."

How to find the missing old lady was a problem which perplexed Nancy. She knew that probably the woman was in Sea Cliff; otherwise Joe Mitza could not keep in touch with her. Yet general inquiry had revealed no clue as to the old lady's whereabouts.

"Perhaps Dad can help me find her," Nancy thought. Turning round, she hurried back to Brighton Baths.

Upon coming within view of the automobile she saw that Mr Trixler was seated in the car, evidently having waited for several minutes. He was not in as good humour as usual, for due to the carelessness of a bath attendant he had slipped on a cake of soap.

"Drat this place," he complained loudly to George and Bess. "I come here to be helped and they make me a lot worse! They take my money and try to cripple me for life! I've a mind to sue 'em, that's what!"

Nancy came hurrying up to the car, apologizing because she had kept the party waiting.

"It doesn't matter," Mr Trixler answered, for he was fond of the girl, and never spoke crossly to her even in an unpleasant mood.

Nancy hurriedly started the car and drove slowly back towards Sea Cliff. At the Seaside Hotel, Mr Trixler was deposited at the front door, while the Drew girl and her chums took the auto to the garage.

"I suppose we could go for a little drive," George suggested indifferently. "We have the car to ourselves now."

Nancy shook her head.

"I don't want to go anywhere until after I've had a chance to talk with Dad."

"Anything wrong?" George inquired quickly. During the drive from Brighton Baths she had thought Nancy strangely quiet and tense. Now, as they walked back to the hotel, the latter revealed everything she had over-heard in the pine woods.

"Why, Mitza should be turned over to the police!" Bess exclaimed indignantly. "I have never heard of a more contemptible trick—stealing from an old lady."

"Miss Morse must be found and warned," Nancy

said soberly. "She told me to keep out of her affairs, but I feel I shouldn't, knowing what I do."

"Joe Mitza is too clever for her," George replied. "If you stop him stealing the money, Miss Morse should be highly grateful, Nancy."

"She should be—yes. But Miss Morse is a peculiar type. I'm not expecting any thanks, but I don't want to see her cheated."

The girls went into the hotel. In the foyer, the desk clerk signalled to Nancy.

"I have a message for you," he declared, offering a sealed letter.

"Why, this is in Dad's handwriting," Nancy murmured in surprise.

She ripped open the envelope and quickly scanned the brief missive.

"Oh, girls, this is disappointing. Dad has left Sea Cliff."

"He hasn't gone back to River Heights, has he?" Bess inquired with concern, fearing that the end of their own vacation might be in sight.

"No, he has been called away on business to an inland city not far from here, a place named Bardwell. He expects to be back in a day or two. But that may be too late."

"What will you do, Nancy?" Bess asked.

"I scarcely know what course to follow," the girl admitted, frowning. "I counted upon Dad's advice."

"How about trying some of mine?" demanded a masculine voice.

Nancy and her chums whirled round to see Mr Trixler standing behind them.

"Perhaps you can help us," Nancy said eagerly, for

she felt she could trust the old gentleman. "But we can't talk here."

Finding a deserted nook of the foyer, she then told the invalid about the urgent necessity for locating Miss Morse.

"There's only one thing to do, of course," the old gentleman said promptly when he learned of Joe Mitza's scheme to defraud the woman. "The police should be notified."

"I suppose it would be wise," Nancy admitted thoughtfully. "But I wonder if my testimony will be sufficient to hold Mitza and that man named Burne?"

"It ought to be. Anyway, if Mitza should be questioned by the police he'd be afraid to go on with his scheme even if he were released."

"That's true," Nancy agreed.

"I'll go talk to the police myself," Mr Trixler offered chivalrously. "Just leave everything to me. This is a man's affair, anyway," he added with a laugh, "and I'm feeling well enough for a little exercise."

After Nancy had permitted the old man to go alone to the station house, she began to regret that she had not accompanied him.

"I'm afraid he'll not be able to make the story sound convincing," she told her chums.

Mr Trixler was gone for more than an hour. When he returned, the girls could tell by the expression of his face that the mission had not been a satisfactory one.

"Drat that stupid chief of police!" he complained angrily. "Not an ounce of brains in his thick skull!"

"Didn't he believe the story?" Nancy asked.

"I don't know what he thought," Mr Trixler growled. "He just sat there and looked at me and didn't say much except that no one by the name of Fanny Morse ever lived here."

"Whichever way we turn, we always run into that peculiar fact," Nancy replied slowly. "She *must* live here. Didn't the police even promise to question Mitza?"

"They said they'd look him up, but I doubt if they'll exert themselves that much."

It was clear to Nancy that the police had taken Mr Trixler to be an obsessed old fellow and thus had discredited his story. She considered making a trip to police headquarters herself, but decided that it would do no good.

"Apparently the only thing for us to do is to find Miss Morse ourselves," she said, thinking aloud.

"I intend to talk to the police again," Mr Trixler fumed. "I'll make 'em do something."

More than ever, did Nancy wish that her father were there. While Mr Trixler meant well, she did not believe that he would be of great aid in locating Miss Morse or in accomplishing the arrest of Mitza and his companion. Later in the afternoon when the girls went to the bathing beach for a swim, she became very quiet.

"Oh, why not forget Miss Morse?" Bess urged her chum. "You've done everything you can."

"She wasn't a bit nice to you on the train," George added. "You'll ruin the entire vacation worrying about her."

Nancy laughed good-naturedly, and after that dutifully made a special effort to be gay. She raced her chums to the float, winning out by several strokes. After resting awhile, the girls swam back to shore and buried themselves in the warm sand.

"Let's rent a rowboat," George proposed suddenly.

"We can hire one for twenty-five cents an hour."

"It will be hard to row in the high waves," Nancy remarked, turning to stare at the sea.

However, George and Bess were so eager for the little adventure that she offered no serious objection. The boatman appeared a trifle hesitant about renting them a craft.

"Are you all good swimmers?" he inquired dubiously.

"Oh, yes," Bess laughed. "Haven't you ever heard about our swimming the English Channel?"

"No," the man responded dryly, "but I've fished out plenty of persons who drowned because they were too confident. The water is treacherous."

"We'll be careful," Bess promised, growing grave.

"Watch out for the turn of the tide," the man warned again, as he helped the girls to launch the boat.

As they rowed away, they saw him watching them anxiously. Then, apparently satisfied that they knew how to handle the oars, he turned away.

"This isn't as much fun as I thought it would be," George presently complained as she tugged at the oars. "It's more like plain hard work."

The water was so rough that the boat rocked unpleasantly and George had difficulty in steering it where she wished. They rode the crest of a wave, then plunged down into a trough.

"I think we ought to go back," Nancy said anxiously, gazing towards the beach some distance away. "The lifeguards are making all the swimmers leave the water."

"The water is getting rougher," Bess added. "Probably a storm is brewing."

"Oh, I'm ready to turn back," George said, swerving the boat by pulling on her right oar. "I've had enough."

Nancy's alert eyes were sweeping the dark water. A short distance away, there was a lone swimmer who evidently had been too far from the beach to hear the whistle of the lifeguards.

"Why doesn't that fellow turn back?" she murmured anxiously. "He may be carried out to sea."

"Perhaps we ought to warn him," George replied, and at Nancy's nod she steered towards the young man.

"Look!" cried Bess an instant later.

Her gaze was riveted upon a great wall of water which was travelling swiftly towards them. Before the girls could shout a warning to the swimmer, the huge wave struck the boat and raised it high. Then the craft plunged down into a trough.

Nancy glanced anxiously about for the young man. She could not see him anywhere.

"He has gone down!" she gasped in panic.

"No, there he is!" George shouted excitedly. "He's caught in the undertow!"

Following George's frightened gaze, Nancy and Bess saw the swimmer battle frantically and then suddenly give up. They feared that he would sink before they could reach him.

"The man is weakening," Nancy observed. "Give the oars everything you have, George!"

·7·   Old Estate

BEFORE the boat could reach the swimmer, he went under. Nancy stood poised, ready to dive into the turbulent water after him if necessary. He reappeared at the surface again, but seemed unable to help himself.

"Don't give up!" she shouted encouragingly, then added to her chums, "He has cramp, I guess."

George finally brought the boat alongside so that the other girls could grasp the young man by his bathing suit. They tried to pull him aboard, but it was difficult to do so. Nancy was afraid that in such rough water the boat would upset if it became even slightly over-balanced.

"Can you hold on to the side for a few minutes?" she asked the swimmer. "We'll tow you ashore."

Exhausted as he was, the dark-haired youth still was able to flash Nancy a courageous grin. While she and Bess held fast to the young man, George rowed as rapidly as she could towards shore. When they reached shallow water, several lifeguards came wading out to assist.

"I'm all right now," the rescued swimmer chattered in protest. "Just give me something warm to drink."

"You're lucky you didn't drown," the lifeguard growled. "What was the idea, not coming in when I gave the signal?"

"I didn't hear you," the young man returned, slipping into a bathrobe which was held for him. "Then I got cramp and in the undertow I couldn't do a thing for myself. Say, where are those girls who hauled me in? I want to talk to them."

Nancy, Bess and George were standing at the edge of the crowd which had gathered. They felt a trifle embarrassed, for everyone seemed to be staring at them and pointing them out as heroines. They were glad that the young man did not appear to have suffered any ill effects from his unpleasant experience. When he attempted to express his appreciation they tried to pass the matter off lightly.

"My name is Jack Kingdon," he told them, and his smile was most attractive. "I'm so cold I can't talk without my teeth rattling together just now, but you'll hear from me again."

The girls thought no more about the remark, for they had not even told the young man their names. A few minutes later as they were leaving the beach after changing their clothes, a well-dressed woman of early middle age approached them.

"Aren't you the girls who rescued my son?" she inquired with a smile. "I am Mrs Kingdon."

When Nancy and her chums admitted that they were, the woman thanked them profusely. She concluded by saying cordially:

"I should be delighted to have you take luncheon with me tomorrow at my cottage. Jack is so eager to know you better."

The girls were overjoyed to receive the invitation and promptly accepted it. The following afternoon found them rapping on the door of a picturesque cottage by the ocean. Mrs Kingdon admitted them herself before the maid could answer the summons.

"Luncheon will be served soon," she smiled after she had taken their coats and made them welcome. "Until then you might enjoy wandering round the garden with Jack."

Mrs Kingdon's son, immaculately dressed, was even more handsome and charming than the girls had thought him. He was a perfect host, escorting them through the old-fashioned flower garden and telling them many things of interest concerning Sea Cliff.

"Have you lived here all your life?" Bess inquired.

"Oh, no, but Mother and I usually spend our summers at Sea Cliff. We've been coming here to this same cottage off and on for eight years—ever since I was a little boy."

"Do you happen to know anyone named Fanny Morse living here?" Nancy inquired quickly.

Jack Kingdon repeated the name and shook his head.

"I can't seem to find anyone who has ever heard of her," Nancy sighed. "Or for that matter, of the 'Whispering Girl' statue."

" 'The Whispering Girl'," Jack repeated in surprise. "Why, I know about that . . . I've seen it."

"Tell me where it is located," Nancy pleaded eagerly.

"Why, not far from here on the old Conger estate. Old Estate some persons call it, though usually it goes under the other name. The property is abandoned now and is rapidly falling into decay."

"I'd give anything to see the statue," Nancy told him. "I've been told that I bear a slight resemblance to the marble figure."

Jack stared at her face.

"Why, so you do! It's uncanny! I say, after lunch let's drive over to Old Estate and you can see the statue yourself."

Nancy and her chums said that they could think of nothing they would like better. During luncheon, Mrs Kingdon was able to tell the girls additional facts about the abandoned property.

"The place originally belonged to a wealthy man named Conger, I believe," she explained. "He was respected in the community, but unfortunately he had a daughter who was rather wild. She ran away from home when she was very young and married a worthless fellow—I don't recall that I ever heard his name.

"At any rate, the man turned out to be a criminal, leading the girl into evil ways. She was arrested once for theft, but Mr Conger fixed matters up somehow. Yet according to rumour it cost him a great deal."

"I should have thought he would have preferred to disown his daughter," Bess remarked.

"Mr Conger was devoted to the girl. Whenever she was in trouble, she appealed to him for help, and he never failed her. In the end it cost him his health, home and happiness. He allowed Old Estate to fall into ruin because he could not afford to repair it or build a retaining wall to keep the sea from washing away the property."

"No one has lived at the place for years," Jack added. "Not since Mr Conger died. Every winter the water has been cutting deeper and deeper into the land, and any day I expect to hear that the house has toppled into the sea."

"It will probably go the first time we have a severe storm," Mrs Kingdon declared. "A pity, too, for years ago the place was one of the most attractive at Sea Cliff."

Soon after luncheon, as he had promised, Jack drove the girls to Old Estate. An ancient gate still barred the entrance to the winding private road which led to the house. As the young man pulled it open so that they might drive through, a loose board fell to the ground, making it impossible to close the barrier again. The road was dry but rutty, and a wild jungle of shrubs brushed against the car as it passed.

"Whatever became of Mr Conger's daughter?" George inquired curiously as the auto bounced along.

Jack shrugged. "No one ever knew. After her last trouble with the police, she disappeared and was never heard of again. She did not return home even for her father's funeral."

"That was gratitude," Bess murmured, "especially when the old man sacrificed his entire fortune for her."

The automobile rounded a bend and halted before a weather-beaten, rambling old house which was perched high above the sea. It stood at a rakish angle, since one wing had no form of support at all. The water had cut a great tunnel beneath it.

"Another season, and the house surely will topple into the sea," Jack declared, gazing about him with interest. "A lot of damage has been done since last I visited here."

Towards the right lay what remained of a garden. There were a few scraggly rose bushes entangled among a jungle of weeds. Yet when the visitors came within view of the Whispering Girl statue, they halted and stared in awe, for the figure tended to dignify its unkempt surroundings.

The marble piece was still imposing, though weather-beaten and old. The group consisted of three sculptured figures; a life-sized likeness of a beautiful girl with flowing hair, on either side of which, at a little distance, stood a smaller statue. The central figure bore a startling resemblance to Nancy.

"Why, Mrs Owen was right," Bess murmured when she found her voice. "You're enough like that statue, Nancy, to be its twin!"

"It makes me feel sort of creepy to see myself reflected

in marble," her chum admitted as the young people moved forward to inspect the piece at close range.

Jack had brought his camera and now took several snapshots of Nancy standing beside the Whispering Girl. He promised that he would send prints of the pictures to her when they should be developed.

"Do you know the history of the statue, Jack?" Nancy inquired curiously.

"Only in a general way. The marble was imported from Italy, I've been told, and is of the best quality. I have never heard who the sculptor was."

"I suppose the statue received its name from the peculiar pose of the central figure," Nancy said musingly.

"Undoubtedly," agreed Jack. "I'm sure the marble never talks!"

"Listen!" Nancy commanded suddenly.

Everyone remained quiet for a moment. Save for the whistle of the wind in the pine boughs and the roar of the ocean, there was no other sound.

"One can almost imagine that the statue is whispering now," Nancy murmured.

"It's only the wind," George Fayne said impatiently.

"Of course," Nancy returned quickly, "and I hope you won't think me superstitious, but I find the illusion almost perfect."

"I imagine if one were here on a stormy night the old statue would practically howl!" Bess laughed.

"I doubt if it will be here much longer," Nancy said regretfully. "It stands so close to the bank that when the house goes it may sink out of sight. What a pity!"

"I think I'll go round to the ocean side of the building," said Jack Kingdon, "and take some more pictures. You're not in a hurry, are you?"

"No," replied Nancy. "We'll wait here. Take as much time as you like."

The truth is that the girl was so fascinated by the statue that she was not ready to leave the spot yet. A few minutes after the young man had disappeared from view, the attention of Nancy and her chums was diverted by the sound of screeching brakes. A large truck had come to an abrupt stop in the driveway. A swarthy, heavy-set foreigner climbed from the cab, approaching the group with quick, hurried steps.

"You own-a da place?" he questioned Nancy, his manner eager and impatient.

"No, I do not," the girl replied emphatically.

Ignoring her denial, and speaking rapidly, the man told Nancy that he was a contractor. He would like the job of wrecking the old mansion and disposing of the marble statues.

"I can't give you permission to dismantle the place," Nancy said firmly.

"I do-a good work," he insisted. "I no cheat. I honest man. When I make-a da promise, my word fine."

"I'm not doubting your integrity at all," Nancy replied, somewhat amused at the man's insistence. "I don't own the place so I couldn't possibly give the job to you."

It was evident that the contractor thought Nancy was merely endeavouring to drive a hard bargain. Despite the girl's repeated denials he could not believe that she was not the owner of the property, for the statue resembled her.

"I give five hundred dollar. You get no better price."

Nancy wearily shook her head.

"You shake-a da head but I make what you say—

deduction, yes? Da statue is made for you: your lips; your cheeks; your mouth. It is da same."

"The statue may look a little like me but that doesn't mean the estate is mine."

The man still was not satisfied, but he was diverted from further questioning by the sudden appearance of his pet monkey which had escaped from its tether in the truck. Instead of seeking its master, however, the little animal espied the tall porch pillars of the ancient house. With astonishing agility he shot up one of them and squatted down near a window on the roof.

His master grew very excited. He scolded the monkey in broken English and then tried his native tongue, but the little fellow did not choose to understand. Instead, Jocko cowered by the window and looked up the side of the house, seeking further elevations to scale.

Suddenly the man seized a rock and hurled it at his escaped pet. The missile flew wide of its mark and crashed through the window, glass flying in all directions. Suddenly the monkey vanished.

"Oh, he crawled through the broken window," cried George. The girl laughed as she watched the angry contractor shake his fist at the vanished pet.

"I get you! I get you!" he shrieked. "And when I do, Jocko, of you I make-a da hash!"

·8· *Locating Miss Morse*

THE contractor ran round the house, searching for some means of entrance, but found all the doors and windows locked. As the man could not scale the porch column as Jocko had done, he muttered impatiently to himself, and then sat down to wait until the monkey should reappear.

Nancy and her chums wished to help the man recover his pet but without a ladder there was nothing they could do. Bess wandered round the outside of the house trying the windows herself to make certain the fellow had not overlooked any of them. Towards the rear she found one where a shutter had been left open.

"Take a look inside, girls," she invited. "Some of the furniture is still in the house."

"Imagine that!" Bess exclaimed. "After all these years!"

"I wonder why it was never taken away," Nancy mused as she joined her chums at the window.

Peering into the darkened interior, the girls made out several massive pieces of furniture draped with ghostly sheets and protecting covers. A grand piano stood at the far end of the room into which they gazed.

Suddenly Nancy and her chums were startled to hear the roar of the Italian's truck. They ran to the road.

"I go now," the man shouted above the noise of the motor. "I gotta no time to wait for Jocko."

Before anyone could protest, the contractor had driven away.

"What will become of the poor little monkey?" Nancy worried. "He'll starve if he's left in that house."

Jack Kingdon appeared at this moment and was told what had happened.

"The contractor will probably come back later for his pet," he assured the girls.

The young people waited for nearly half an hour,

hoping that the animal would reappear at the window. Finally, since it was growing late, they were compelled to leave the estate. Jack drove the girls to their hotel. As he left them, he extended a cordial invitation for them to visit the Kingdon cottage again.

Nancy hoped that during her absence Mr Trixler might have gained some information regarding Miss Morse's whereabouts, but she was disappointed to learn that such was not the case. Mr Drew had not returned from his out-of-town business trip, either.

As the girls went to their room to change their clothes, Nancy remarked anxiously, "I wish we hadn't gone away and left Jocko at Old Estate."

"There was nothing we could do," George replied. "It was impossible to get into the house without smashing a window."

"I'd not enjoy prowling about that creepy place anyhow," added Bess. "It was all right going there with Jack, but I shouldn't want to try it alone."

Nancy said nothing. Half an hour later, while her chums were occupied with letter writing, she quietly left the hotel. Making use of Mr Trixler's car, she sought the home of the contractor, finding it after considerable delay and inquiry. The man was not at home, however, and his wife spoke very little English. She was able, fortunately, to make Nancy understand that Jocko had not been recovered from the old deserted house.

"I'm going back there alone to see if I can find him," the Drew girl decided, as she drove towards the country. "I'll never have a peaceful moment until I do."

En route to Old Estate she stopped at a roadside stand to purchase a bag of peanuts. Thus fortified to entice the monkey, she took up her position not far from the

Whispering Statue. There was no sign of the little animal anywhere about the premises.

"Jocko! Jocko!" Nancy called in wheedling tones.

She scarcely expected that the pet would heed her cries. Great was her surprise when she spied him looking down at her from the attic window ledge. Over and over, Nancy pleaded with the little fellow to come down. He eyed her intently but would not obey.

Deciding that the monkey was afraid of her because she was a stranger, Nancy moved back behind the marble statue, leaving a trail of peanuts in her wake. Half-hidden from view, she then called Jocko in whispered tones.

At first the little animal remained indifferent to her calls, but when she was upon the verge of giving up he suddenly swung down the porch pillar and began to gather up the peanuts. Closer and closer he came to Nancy until she was able to reach out and grab him. Jocko squirmed in her grasp, but as soon as he discovered there were more peanuts to be had, he slipped a paw about the girl's neck and was content to be carried away.

As Nancy hurried with the monkey to the car, a taxi cab came up the driveway. She was dumbfounded to see Bess, George and Mr Trixler alight.

"I thought we'd find you here," George declared as they came towards Nancy. "Bess and I were almost certain you'd come back looking for that monkey."

"I was just about to take Jocko home," said Nancy.

For a moment, she wondered if Mr Trixler were provoked at her for using his car; yet she knew that such hardly could be the case, for he had urged her many times to take it whenever she wished to do so.

"We have interesting news for you!" Bess declared, her eyes bright with excitement. "Mr Trixler has located Miss Morse."

"Oh, where is she?" Nancy cried in delight.

"The police tell me she's staying at a tourist camp," Mr Trixler explained. "It's called the Sunset Camp."

"The hotel people gave us the suitcase she left in our room," Bess went on. "We thought we'd take it to her but we didn't want to go without you."

Nancy was grateful that Mr Trixler and the girls had gone to so much trouble to find her, for she would have been bitterly disappointed had they made the trip without her. They dismissed the taxi, and everyone rode in Mr Trixler's car to the Sunset Tourist Camp, located only a few miles farther on. Driving up to the little office at the entrance of the park, Nancy explained to the man in charge that they wished to see a camper by the name of Miss Morse.

"Cottage 16," he directed gruffly.

She drove through the gateway, parking in front of a two-room overnight cabin.

"I scarcely know how I'll be received," Nancy whispered to her chums.

Leaving the active Jocko in George's care, she took out Miss Morse's suitcase. Setting it down by the cottage door she rapped lightly. It was opened almost at once by a middle-aged woman wearing a pink house dress.

As Nancy gazed fixedly at her, the girl did not notice a small boy who emerged from an adjoining cabin and stared curiously at the bag. He sidled near by and began to examine the suitcase.

"I was told that Miss Morse resides in this cottage," said Nancy to the woman.

"I am Miss Morse."

Nancy could not hide her disappointment. She had expected to meet the old lady of the black cloak, but obviously there were two persons in Sea Cliff by the same name. She explained about the bag having been left by mistake in her room at the Seaside Hotel.

"I've lost no luggage," the woman replied, glancing at the suitcase. "I never owned one like that, either."

Unnoticed by Nancy, the small boy had been tampering with the fastenings of the case. At a sharp word from Miss Morse he scuttled away.

"That child next door is a dreadful pest," the woman apologized. "Always prying into things."

Nancy laughed good-naturedly and reached down to pick up the bag. As she lifted it, the lid fell back.

A small black box which appeared to be a make-up kit tumbled to the ground, and with it a woman's blond wig. The clothing which lay exposed was of the latest style, and of a type usually worn by young women.

"Well, mercy sakes," Miss Morse murmured in astonishment. "I guess the owner of that bag must be an actress!"

·9· *At the Carnival*

NANCY hastily replaced the wig and make-up kit in the bag and closed down the lid. To the comment of the woman that the owner of the suitcase must be an actress, she was tempted to add:

"Either that, or else a person travelling in disguise."

"We made a trip all for nothing," Bess murmured as her chum climbed in and took her place at the steering wheel. "What was it that fell from the bag, Nancy? You snatched it up so quickly that we couldn't see what it was."

"A wig and a make-up kit. As soon as we're out of the park I hope to get a better look at them because I can't understand why Miss Morse would carry such articles."

Once she was out on the main road, Nancy drew up under a tree. She reopened the suitcase and showed Mr Trixler and her chums the strange contents. Although the girls felt confident that the bag belonged to the mysterious woman of the black cape, they could find no papers or evidence to identify it as hers except for the tag on the outside of the case. All markings had been removed from the clothing.

"What do you make of it, Nancy?" George inquired in a baffled tone.

"The only way I can figure it out is that Miss Morse sometimes travels in disguise, but just why should she do such a thing? I confess it's too deep a mystery for me."

"I never heard you say such a thing before," Bess teased. "I'll warrant you'll have the answer to the riddle before we leave Sea Cliff."

"How can I when Dad is due to return any minute now? Probably we'll start for home soon after he comes. If I could only locate Miss Morse I'd have a definite place to begin—but as it is, I'm baffled."

"Probably Mitza has the five thousand dollars by this time anyway," George remarked.

"I doubt it, George," said Nancy, shaking her head. "Miss Morse isn't as stupid as Mitza assumed. Now that

I've seen the contents of this suitcase I'm wondering if perhaps she won't prove a match for him."

"Well, if we can't find the woman, we just can't," Mr Trixler next said philosophically. "At least we have the satisfaction of knowing we tried to expose a trickster."

As far as Nancy was concerned, to have tried and failed was no satisfaction at all. She resolved that she would never give up the search for Miss Morse until the hour she stepped on the train to return home.

En route back to the hotel, the girls left Jocko at the house of his master. They received the gratitude of the contractor's entire family, which was considerable in number. They were glad to be relieved of the pet for his mischievous inclinations were not unlike those of Togo.

At the hotel, the girls found a note left by Jack Kingdon, requesting them to attend a carnival that evening. They lost no time telephoning to say that they would be delighted to accept the invitation.

Soon after dinner, the young people arrived at the scene of the street fair, mingling with the gay crowd which wandered from one stand to another. Jack bought popcorn and candy for the girls and encouraged them to try their luck at various games of chance. His supply of nickels and dimes seemed inexhaustible.

"You've been spending all your money on us," Nancy protested finally. "Why not try some of the games yourself?"

"Perhaps I will," Jack smiled. "We're coming to the shooting gallery, and it's always hard for me to pass by one of those."

They paused to watch the moving row of targets and Jack stepped forward to pick up one of the rifles. Not until then did the girls notice a man who was firing at some clay ducks, his back towards them. Nancy was the first to recognize him.

"Joe Mitza!" she whispered.

"It is!" Bess agreed excitedly. "Will you try to have him arrested, Nancy?"

"I'm afraid I haven't enough evidence to hold him, Bess. But I intend to ask him where I can find Miss Morse."

She waited until the man laid the rifle down on the counter. Then, as he was turning away from the gallery, she stepped forward. As she spoke, Mitza stared at her sharply. For an instant his expression was blank; then a hard, cunning look in his eyes told Nancy that he recognized her.

"How do you do?" she began with a pretence of politeness. "I am very eager to find a certain Miss Morse——"

"I never heard of her," the man interrupted harshly.

"The old lady in the black cape. You were so friendly with her on the train that I thought you might know her address here in Sea Cliff."

"Well, I don't."

"Her suitcase was delivered to me by mistake," Nancy continued, "and that's why I wish to reach her."

At mention of the bag a flicker of interest came into Mitza's crafty eyes, but in an instant it was gone.

"Sorry, but I can't help you," he answered shortly, turning away.

As Mitza mingled with the crowd again, Nancy gripped Jack Kingdon by the arm.

"Do you mind leaving the carnival?" she requested. "I must find out where that fellow is staying here in Sea Cliff."

"Then we'll follow him," Jack declared promptly.

It was not difficult to keep Mitza in sight for he walked slowly, pausing at various stands. Hovering always in the background, Nancy and her chums noted that the man lost money heavily. Presently he left the carnival grounds.

The young people followed him to a cheap boarding house on a squalid street by the railroad tracks. By interviewing the landlady, they learned that for several days past Mitza had been rooming with a friend. Nancy carefully noted the address.

Then, since it was too late to go back to the carnival, the four returned to the hotel. Nancy was delighted to find that during their absence her father had arrived.

"You look very tired, Dad," she observed after he had kissed her fondly. "Have a good trip?"

"Just fair. I'm glad to be back. Oh, yes, I brought you a little present."

"You needn't have done that, Dad."

"This is really from my client," her father smiled. "Perhaps you won't care for it."

He unwrapped a small package, holding up several yards of rich brocade in a curious and unusual flowered pattern.

"Why, it's gorgeous, Dad!" Nancy cried in admiration.

"I don't know what you'll ever be able to do with it."

"Leave that to me," the girl laughed. "I can think of several uses for such beautiful material."

Then and there, she determined to make her father a necktie as a surprise, but she gave no hint as to what was in her mind. Instead she asked:

"Where did you get the cloth, Dad?"

"Why, from my client, Mr Owen. It came from the firm's warehouse."

"I didn't know you had gone out of town to see Mr Owen," Nancy remarked with interest.

"It's a badly muddled case," Mr Drew remarked half to himself. Then, as was frequently his custom, he began to discuss the details aloud. "You see, some years ago Charles Owen entered into a partnership with a man by the name of Frank Wormrath. The two men never got along very well together and Owen began to distrust his partner. One night the firm's warehouse was broken into and valuable stock consisting of silk and woollen goods was stolen. The thefts never were traced.

"Soon after that, Wormrath broke up the partnership. What puzzled Owen was that although the profits of the firm had never been large, Wormrath suddenly seemed well supplied with money and a fine stock of goods with which to start another company in competition."

"Did Mr Owen connect it with the warehouse theft?" Nancy speculated shrewdly.

"Yes, he became convinced that his partner had instigated the thefts in order to gain a valuable share of the stock of goods—more than he would have been entitled to when a split-up might come."

"And how do you figure in the case, Dad?" Nancy questioned. "Were you engaged to uncover damaging evidence against Wormrath?"

"Yes, I've gone through hundreds of documents with just fair success. I've gleaned a little information, but the fellow was shrewd. He evidently confined his dishonest activities to this one big theft."

"Will you go back to see Mr Owen?"

"I may return to Windham in a few days," Mr Drew answered, "although I can't see just what good I can do. There's nothing more I can glean from the records of the firm. But don't look so worried, Nancy. This is my case, not yours, so you're not to lose any sleep over it."

"I never lose sleep over any case," Nancy laughed. "But I am worried about you. Dad, you look positively worn out."

"I look the way I feel. But I'll be all right soon. I've just been grinding a bit too hard."

"What you need, Dad, is a good brisk swim."

"Not at this time of night."

"It will do you good and make you sleep better," Nancy urged. "The moon is full, too, and the beach will be beautiful. I'll go with you."

"Oh, all right," Carson Drew agreed unwillingly.

However, after a ten-minute dip in the bracing sea he was glad he had listened to his daughter's plea, for he felt alive in every part of his lean body. He raced Nancy back to the dressing room.

"And now to bed and to sleep," he declared a few minutes later, kissing her good night.

Bess and George already were in bed. Nancy tiptoed across the room, and without disturbing them she began to take off her shoes. She was startled to hear a soft knock on the door.

"Who is it?" she asked, slipping her shoes back on again.

She felt reassured when she heard her father's voice. He asked her to step out into the hall for a minute and she obeyed immediately.

"What is it, Dad? You look upset."

"Come into my room so we'll not be heard," he urged in a whisper.

She followed her father, who closed the door behind them.

"Nancy, you didn't pick up my briefcase just before we went for our swim, did you?"

"Why no. I think I saw you drop it on the dresser."

Nancy's eyes wandered to the bureau which now bore only a few toilet articles.

"I was afraid of it," Mr Drew murmured in agitation. "While we were away someone stole the case, and it contained valuable private papers."

·10·   *A Significant Clue*

"PERHAPS you only misplaced the briefcase, Dad," Nancy said hopefully. "It should be here somewhere."

"It should be but it isn't," Carson Drew replied grimly. "No, I'm convinced the case has been stolen. I have an idea that the thief, whoever he is, came here knowing where I had the Owen-Wormrath papers. It will be a blow to have the documents lost or get into the hands of someone against my client's interests."

Nancy searched the room carefully but the missing briefcase could not be found. Suddenly she stooped to pick up a brown button from the floor. A glance assured her that it did not belong to her father's suit.

"Let me see that," Mr Drew said quickly. "I believe you've found a clue, Nancy."

"This button must have come from the thief's coat,"

Nancy declared, proud that she had observed something which her keen-eyed father had overlooked. "It may help to identify him later."

"Yes, if we are able to trace the man," Carson Drew nodded. "I will question the maids."

Inquiry revealed that neither the cleaning women who served the floor nor any of the bellboys had seen any suspicious looking person in the vicinity of Mr Drew's room. The hotel manager, although disturbed over the theft, was likewise unable to be of any help.

Nancy and the lawyer returned to their own floor, discouraged at their failure to find additional clues. Mr Drew paused in the hall for a moment to get a cool drink of water from an ice tank. Walking slowly on alone, Nancy rounded a corner of the corridor where she paused abruptly.

The Drew girl had seen a shadowy form move hastily away from her father's room. She could not be certain, but she believed the man had been listening at the door. He walked rapidly, and without glancing backward entered his own room at the end of the hall.

When Mr Drew joined her Nancy told him what she had observed. The lawyer was inclined to believe that the man she had seen was merely curious, having no connection whatsoever with the theft of the briefcase.

"Don't lose any sleep over the matter," he said kindly. "Go to bed now and in the morning we can delve deeper into the affair."

Nancy retired but could not fall asleep. She knew that her father was deeply concerned over the loss of the papers and wished that she might aid him in recovering them.

"I believe that man who was skulking at the door did

have something to do with the theft," she thought. "I wish I could have caught a glimpse of his face."

In the morning Nancy woke with a firm determination to try out a little scheme of her own. Telling Bess and George she would not eat breakfast with them, she waited in her room until they had gone downstairs. Then she raced to a nearby shop she had noticed previously and purchased a chambermaid's uniform. Hurriedly she returned and changed her clothes.

"I look the part, I'm sure," she said, glancing at herself in the mirror.

Gathering up several clean towels, she opened the door of her room. No one was in the hall, so she hastened along the corridor until she reached the spot where she had seen the suspicious stranger go the night before. Rapping on number 359, she waited.

"Who's there?" a gruff voice demanded.

Nancy did not dare reply, as she had no master key with which to open the door. Finally the occupant of the room strode across the carpet and in a moment was facing the maid.

"May I make the bed now?" Nancy asked sweetly.

"Oh, I suppose so," the man growled. "Come on in."

The girl's heart began to beat a little faster as she directed a swift, searching glance at the man. He was an unpleasant looking individual with a sharp, evil face. She had never seen him before. He sat down at once at a desk to continue writing a letter.

"Try not to make a lot of clatter," he said irritably.

"Yes, sir, I'll work very quietly," Nancy murmured meekly, beginning to dust the place which was a sitting room. All the while her eyes were roving swiftly about in search of her father's briefcase.

"Can't you let that go?" the man demanded with a scowl after a few moments.

"I'll do the other room first, sir," Nancy offered.

"All right, I wish you would. Clear out of here. But mind you don't bother any of my private papers."

"Oh, no," Nancy murmured again.

She slipped quietly into the next room and shook the bed several times, causing the springs to rattle so that the man would assume that she was busy with sheets and blankets. Then she moved stealthily to the bureau and softly opened each drawer.

"Empty," she observed in disappointment.

Next the clothes closet drew her attention. She saw a suitcase full of wearing apparel, and beside it was her father's briefcase!

Fearing that she might not be able to take it from the suite without discovery, Nancy quickly divested it of some papers which she stuffed into the front of her uniform.

Scarcely had she done this, when she heard the man in the next room push back his chair and come towards the bed chamber. Swiftly Nancy darted away from the closet. She was deeply engrossed in her bedmaking when he entered.

Ignoring her, he moved to the telephone and called the office. He told the clerk that he was checking out in ten minutes. Nancy went on calmly smoothing the bed covers, but her mind worked with lightning rapidity. Unless she acted quickly, the fellow would escape from the hotel. He must be detained at all costs.

Nancy knew that she had located the thief, for in addition to the incriminating briefcase she noticed that the top button of the man's coat was missing.

She held her breath when he went to the closet for his luggage. However, he picked up the bag and the brief-case without opening the latter. When a bellboy came to the door a few minutes later he gave up the suitcase but insisted upon carrying the briefcase himself. The instant the door closed, Nancy darted to the telephone.

"Detain the man from Room 359 who is just coming down to pay his bill," she said crisply to the clerk. "He is carrying away stolen property."

Then hastening back to her room, Nancy quickly changed into her normal clothing. She called her father from the adjoining suite and told him of her discovery. He identified readily the papers as those which had been stolen.

"Clever work, Nancy," he praised. "We'll go down-stairs and take a look at the thief."

The detained man blustered and fumed.

"It is an outrage to accuse me of stealing it," he retorted angrily. "I found it in my room when I came in late last night. How it got there I don't know, but I assumed it had been left by the former room occupant. At any rate, I was just turning it in here at the desk."

"And can you explain away this button just as readily?" Nancy asked sarcastically.

She held up the brown object so that all might see that it was identical with the others on the man's suit. For an instant the wily individual looked stunned.

"My daughter picked up this button in my room last night," Carson Drew said coldly.

"I don't know anything about it," the accused person muttered, avoiding the lawyer's eyes. He appealed to the hotel clerk. "This man—whoever he is—hasn't a scrap of proof. Are you going to believe his story or mine?"

"Well," the clerk stammered uncomfortably, "the briefcase was found in your room, Mr Dencer——"

"Left there by someone else, I told you. Probably this girl planted it herself just to make trouble for me."

"How ridiculous!" Nancy said. "I suppose you claim I pulled the button off your suit, too!"

"As to the button, it has no significance. The one I lost from my coat has been missing for a month."

The man tossed the leather briefcase down on the desk. Then, picking up his suitcase, he stalked angrily from the foyer.

"Aren't you going to stop him?" Nancy cried, gazing accusingly at the baffled clerk. "He ought to be arrested."

"There really isn't any proof——" the man began apologetically.

"You're afraid to do anything," Carson Drew said sharply. "Why not admit the truth?" Turning to his daughter he said, "Come along, Nancy."

"Oh, Dad," she murmured in distress. "To let that thief get away——"

"I know, Nancy, but if the hotel folks won't support us we'd only cause a scene if we tried to detain him. Anyway, thanks to your quick thinking, I've recovered the missing papers."

"I hope they're all intact."

"I'll check over everything just as soon as I get to my room," Mr Drew declared. "Let's go there now."

A hasty inspection of the documents taken from the briefcase revealed that nothing had been kept by the thief.

"This affair should serve as a warning to me," Nancy's father remarked thoughtfully, his brows knitting in a frown. "I figure that Wormrath sent that man Dencer here to steal the Owen documents. I fear it's only the beginning of trouble."

"But you'll be on your guard after this, Dad."

"I wasn't thinking of myself, Nancy," Mr Drew replied soberly. "I'm worried about Mr Owen. I am afraid that one of these days he may be missing."

·11·   *An Accident at Sea*

"You mean Mr Wormrath may attempt to kidnap Mr Owen?" Nancy gasped, startled.

"When an unscrupulous person finds himself cornered he will attempt almost anything in order to save his own skin," the lawyer responded dryly. "Mr Owen is getting on in years and should have someone to look after him."

"Why not advise him to employ a bodyguard until the trouble blows over?"

"Oh, I have, but his only reply is 'stuff and nonsense.' He can't seem to realize that we're dealing with a dangerous man."

"It's too bad he doesn't live here in Sea Cliff," Nancy remarked. "If he would only come, you could keep an eye on him yourself, Dad, and I might help you!"

"You'd like the job, wouldn't you?" her father teased. "But I'm afraid Mr Owen wouldn't feel flattered if he thought we believed him incapable of looking after himself."

"He needn't know everything," Nancy chuckled.

"Really I wish he would come here, Dad. Then I could find out if he's related to Mrs Owen of River Heights."

"I suspected that was in your mind all the time," laughed her father. "I meant to ask Mr Owen for you, but we were so pressed with business matters that I forgot about it."

"I don't suppose you could bring Mr Owen here?" Nancy asked eagerly. "Would it be possible to let him think you wished to consult him about the case?"

"I'll consider the matter," her father promised with a smile.

At luncheon he told Nancy that he had sent a telegram to the man, requesting him to come immediately to the Seaside Hotel. Before the meal was over, a reply had been received. Mr Owen agreed to make the trip without delay.

"Remember, it was your idea," Mr Drew reminded Nancy, "so when I'm not around you'll be responsible for his safety."

"I'll guard him like a G-man," Nancy promised, laughing. "Bess, George and I will never allow him out of our sight."

Since it was not anticipated that Mr Owen could arrive before the following morning, the girls accepted an invitation from Jack Kingdon to try ocean fishing in his motor boat. They were thrilled at the opportunity, for it would be the first time for that sport.

The day was warm and the water smooth as glass. Jack complained that he was afraid the fish might refuse to strike, but the girls preferred the quiet sea to one which might have made them sick.

Jack was an expert fisherman. He gave each of the girls a huge pole equipped with a large reel and a great length of line, then bated the hooks with raw meat.

"I ought to catch a whale with an outfit like this," George laughed. "What shall I do if I get a strike?"

As the young man had predicted, the fish were not biting. The girls did not mind it, however, for they were enjoying the beautiful day. Presently, a breeze rose and Nancy noticed that the waves were lapping heavily against the boat.

"Looks as if a storm may be kicking up," Jack observed, scanning the clouds.

As he steered towards shore Nancy, hearing a droning noise above, turned her head to watch a passing seaplane. She followed it with her eyes until it was some distance away. Suddenly she gave an excited cry:

"Why, it's landing!"

"And in such rough water!" Bess exclaimed in astonishment. "I should think the pilot would be afraid his machine might upset."

Anxiously, the young people looked on as the plane came down on the surface of the water. It struck heavily, then glided swiftly forward, veering crazily.

"That was a nice landing in such a rough sea," Jack murmured admiringly. "But what's wrong with the pilot? He acts as if he were ill."

"Or else overcome by fumes," Nancy added.

They had seen the aviator slump, one arm dangling over the side. The passenger in the front cockpit signalled frantically to the occupants of the oncoming motor boat, his lips framing words they were unable to hear. They were sure he was calling for help, however.

"We'll be there in a minute," Jack yelled grimly, increasing the speed of the craft.

The boat shot through the water, sending a cold

spray flying into the faces of the girls. Nancy stood beside Jack at the wheel, her eyes glued upon the drifting seaplane. Should it turn broadside to a wave, she feared that the craft might fill up and become submerged.

At that moment she became aware that the pilot and his passenger were in even greater danger. A tongue of flame had shot up suddenly from the fuselage, revealing that fire had caused the forced landing of the ship.

"If the flames reach the gasoline supply it will all be over in a flash!" Jack murmured, his face tense.

Ploughing steadily through the rough water, the motor boat was still some distance from the drifting seaplane. The lone passenger, an elderly man, turned an appealing face towards his would-be rescuers.

"Help! Help!" they heard him call.

"We'll never reach him in time," George murmured anxiously. "The flames are spreading too fast!"

Apparently the passenger was of the same opinion, believing that his only hope of saving himself and the pilot depended upon his own efforts. The young people saw him climb out of the cockpit he was in and struggle frantically to free the unconscious aviator behind him. Finally he succeeded in pushing the man into the sea, then plunged after him.

"They'll both drown!" Bess gasped.

However, the elderly man grasped the pilot by the hair and towed him away from the burning plane. Encumbered by water-soaked clothing and a heavy human weight, he made slight progress in the turbulent sea.

The waves brought the flaming seaplane dangerously close to the men, while each deluge of water which broke over their heads temporarily buried them beneath the surface. The swimmer began to thrash the water and gasp for breath, an indication that he was weakening rapidly.

"That old fellow has courage," Jack muttered. "He won't desert his companion."

"Can't you go faster?" Nancy pleaded.

Jack did not answer, for just at that moment Bess gave a low moan.

"Oh, we're too late. They've gone under!" she cried.

·12·   A Courageous Passenger

A HUGE wave had buried the two men, and it did appear that they had gone under for the last time. But in a moment Nancy and her friends caught a glimpse of a dark head just under the water's surface.

"Can you handle the boat?" Jack asked Nancy tersely.

She nodded and took over the wheel. The young man stood poised at the side, and as the boat made a wide sweep, he dived overboard. He plunged close to the struggling figure which was fighting so valiantly to keep the unconscious pilot afloat. A few powerful strokes brought him to a point directly behind the pair.

Jack grasped the limp body of the aviator, but even when relieved of the burden, the older man seemed scarcely able to battle the heavy waves.

"There is a life-belt under the seat!" Nancy directed George. "Get it quickly!"

The girl flew to obey, and as her chum jockeyed the boat into position, she threw the life preserver towards the struggling man. It fell some feet short, but he was able to swim on until he could grasp the support. He clung tightly to it, gasping for breath.

By this time Nancy had throttled down the motor and was able to bring the boat alongside of Jack and the aviator. The girls pulled the unconscious man aboard, leaving young Kingdon free to return for the exhausted swimmer. In a few minutes the bedraggled pair likewise were pulled aboard.

"Good work, Nancy," Jack murmured admiringly as he took over the wheel again.

Relieved of duty at the helm, Nancy lost no time in attending to the needs of the pilot and his unfortunate passenger. George and Bess were doing the best they could, but were frightened and unable to work calmly.

"Ask Jack if there are any blankets and a first-aid kit aboard," Nancy called, taking command.

One glance assured her that the passenger, though cold and exhausted, required no immediate treatment. It was the pilot who gave her grave concern. She gently removed the heavy headgear which had weighted him down in the water. His face was as white as chalk and he scarcely seemed to breathe.

"Shouldn't we start artificial respiration?" Bess asked anxiously.

Nancy shook her head. "I'll watch his pulse, and unless it gets feebler I don't believe we'll need to do anything more before we get to shore."

"He must have inhaled fumes from the engine in some way," Bess murmured, staring down at the pinched face.

By this time George returned with some blankets and a warm coat for Jack, who was shivering at the wheel. The girls then wrapped up the pilot.

"The fellow appears almost as if he were doped with a drug," Nancy said, half to herself. "I've never before seen anyone look as he does. We must take him to a doctor."

"I'm making full speed ahead for shore," Jack reported grimly.

Finding a thermos bottle of coffee, Nancy urged the old man to take a few sips of it. "It will give you strength and make you feel better," she urged.

He obediently swallowed some of the hot brew, and as the girl slipped an arm about him for support she studied his face. She judged him to be about sixty-two. He had iron grey hair, a kindly countenance, and dark intelligent eyes which denoted quiet courage.

"You were very brave to try saving the pilot," she told him. "But it nearly cost you your own life."

"I couldn't let the fellow go down in that burning plane," the man muttered. "I had to help him."

"What caused the accident?" Nancy asked.

"I don't know. The first thing I realized, the pilot had started to land on the water. Said he felt sick and stupid. We struck heavily, and I guess he fainted before he could flick the switches. Anyway, the machine burst into flames."

"You both had a very narrow escape from death," said Nancy.

"Yes," the elderly man agreed soberly. "We owe our lives to the timely arrival of your motorboat. How is the pilot?"

"He's very ill," Nancy answered. "I can't understand—" Her voice trailed off and she did not mention again that it seemed to her the man might have been drugged.

The motorboat had travelled some distance from the flaming seaplane, but the blaze had attracted the attention of persons on shore. Word went round that a pleasure craft had exploded. The Coast Guards arrived upon the scene, ready to set out for the place of the accident.

At the Seaside Hotel, Carson Drew heard of the occurrence but was unable to learn any of the details. Fearing that Nancy and her friends might have been involved, he ran down to the beach to join the crowd that had gathered there.

Following a record run to shore, the motorboat drew up to the pier. Carson Drew recognized his daughter and tried to push through the excited throng to meet her, but it was several minutes before he could do so. The Coast Guard men, boarding the craft, immediately took charge of the unconscious pilot.

"We'll rush him straight to the hospital," they told Nancy, and added a few words of sincere praise for the young people's rescue work.

"I hope the poor fellow will be all right," Nancy replied anxiously. "I can't understand what is wrong with him."

The Coast Guard men, well trained in all types of first aid, were likewise puzzled by the reaction of the insensible man. However, they offered no opinion. As they left the scene, Mr Drew succeeded in reaching the young people.

"Dad!" Nancy cried joyfully, grasping his hand. "Why, you're trembling!"

"Who wouldn't be?" he demanded gruffly. "I was afraid it was your boat that had blown up. I thought—"

"Mr Carson Drew!" a voice interrupted.

Nancy and her father turned, and saw that the rescued passenger, supported on either side by Jack Kingdon and Bess, had come up directly behind them. He was gazing at the lawyer with an expression of pleased recognition.

For a moment Carson Drew stared blankly.

"Charles Owen!" he exclaimed at last. "I didn't expect you to be in Sea Cliff until tomorrow!"

· 13 ·   *An Act of the Enemy*

"I THOUGHT I'd surprise you and come by plane," Mr Owen returned, smiling. "At the last minute I changed my mind and decided to swim in."

"I took you for an Indian Chief in that blanket," Mr Drew replied in the other's light vein. There his face instantly sobered. "I don't know what happened out there on the water, but I can see you're shivering with cold, Mr Owen. There'll be time enough to talk when we're at the hotel."

He went on ahead, making a pathway through the crowd. The party was rushed to the Seaside Hotel where both the old gentleman and Jack Kingdon were given dry clothing.

Although Mr Owen insisted he felt little the worse for his ducking in the sea, his face was pale, and the young people knew that only his remarkable willpower was sustaining him. The lawyer wisely insisted upon sending the man to bed and calling in a nurse to look after him for a few days.

"I don't need a nurse," the old gentleman complained.

"You're my responsibility here at Sea Cliff," Carson Drew said severely. "I don't want you to die of pneumonia."

"I reckon you couldn't collect your fee then," Mr Owen chuckled, but obediently went to bed.

Nancy remained with the old gentleman until the nurse should arrive, but she could not keep him quiet.

"If the other young lady is half as nice as you, this won't be so bad," he chuckled.

Nancy flushed at the compliment. "You mustn't tire yourself by talking too much," she warned, smiling.

"Maybe I'll tire other folks with my jabbering but not myself. I want to tell you that I appreciate being pulled out of the water, too. I couldn't have held out much longer."

"It was George who tossed you the life preserver," Nancy replied. "But I keep worrying all the time about that poor pilot."

"Yes, it's a mystery to me what was wrong with him," Mr Owen muttered. "He was taken ill so suddenly."

Mr Drew had entered the bedroom again. He pulled up a chair, and at the first opportunity endeavoured to speak seriously to his client.

"You had a fortunate escape from death today, Mr Owen," he began. "Next time you may not be so lucky."

"Next time?" Mr Owen demanded, sitting up very straight against the pillows. "I don't figure there will be a next time. Just what are you driving at, Mr Drew?"

"Has it occurred to you that what happened this afternoon may not have been an accident at all?"

"You think Wormrath was behind it?" the client asked quickly.

"Yes."

"What reason have you for thinking the man would go to such lengths?" Mr Owen questioned.

"Wormrath fears exposure," the lawyer said quietly. "He does not know how much evidence we have against him, and I imagine he believes we are in possession of more than we actually have gathered. Only a day ago my room was entered and valuable papers in this case stolen."

Mr Drew then told how Nancy had recovered the documents from Dencer.

"Wormrath and his hirelings will do anything to prevent the damage suit from coming into court," the lawyer added. "Perhaps I exaggerate, but it is my honest opinion that your life is in danger, Mr Owen."

The elderly man did not speak for several minutes. He seemed to be turning matters over in his mind.

"Perhaps you're right about it, Mr Drew," he admitted slowly. "I've learned that you usually have the correct slant on things. I'll take your advice and be on my guard."

"It means you must remain in your hotel for a few days," advised the lawyer.

Mr Owen made a slight grimace, but promised that he would bide by his friend's judgment. When the nurse came to take charge of the case, Nancy and her father went to the latter's room to talk over matters privately.

"There was every indication, I think," the girl

declared, "that the pilot was doped. I imagine that Wormrath plotted to wreck the plane, thinking that no one ever would be able to prove anything against him."

"I shall investigate that angle thoroughly," Mr Drew nodded. "I'm on my way now to see the doctor who is attending the aviator."

After the lawyer left the hotel, Nancy and her chums found time hanging heavily upon their hands.

"We really should give Togo a little exercise," Nancy remarked. "We've neglected him shamefully the past few days."

"Let's go for a hike now," George proposed impulsively. "We can get back in time for dinner, and there's nothing to do here."

"Haven't you had enough excitement for one day?" Bess asked. She was tired and preferred to remain in her room with a good book.

"Oh, a hike will be good for us all," George laughed. "Come along, lazy."

Selecting a road which took them to the outskirts of Sea Cliff, the girls soon were walking along briskly with Togo scampering ahead of them. He kept tugging impatiently at his leash, so Nancy unfastened it and let the little dog have more freedom.

"He'll probably get into mischief," Bess ventured to say, but Nancy did not feel that it was right to keep the pet confined all the time.

"Oh, Togo is a good dog now," she laughed. "You forget that I've been training him."

"Maybe he will forget it, too," George said dryly.

Presently, the girls approached a tourist camp, and Nancy remarked that it was the one where they had searched for Miss Morse. The place held no interest for them now, and they were just passing by when Nancy suddenly clutched George's hand.

"Isn't that Joe Mitza?" she asked in a whisper, indicating a man who had at that moment entered the park.

Before either George or Bess could catch a glimpse of his face, the fellow moved on through the entrance gate.

"I'm almost certain it was Mitza," Nancy insisted, growing excited. "Come on, girls, let's find out what he is doing here."

The three chums hastened to the entrance of the park in time to see Joe Mitza greet a man who evidently was staying in one of the cabins. The pair sat down on a bench and began to talk.

"Let's steal up behind the cabin and hear what they are saying," Nancy proposed.

The camp was nearly deserted, and no one paid any attention to the girls as they retraced their steps, circled the park, and crept up behind the tourist shack. Mitza was boasting to his friend of various disreputable exploits. As he mentioned Miss Morse's name, a note of complaint came into his harsh voice.

"I figured the old lady was an easy mark, but she fooled me. I thought I had everything lined up to make some money, but yesterday when I went to collect it she said she'd have to do a little more thinking. What I'm trying to decide is whether she's just cautious, or if someone has squealed on me."

"You'll end up in jail one of these days," the other replied shortly.

"Not Joe Mitza!" the fellow boasted. "And I'll get the five thousand from old Miss Morse yet! Maybe I did underestimate her shrewdness, but I'll think up a better scheme next time. You wait and see. I'll have the money jingling round in my pockets before another day passes."

The other man seemed rather unimpressed by Mitza's talk, and Nancy wondered if it might not be because he had listened to the trickster's cheap boasting before.

"The fellow may be only a braggart," she decided. "Since Miss Morse seems well able to take care of herself, there's probably little use in notifying the authorities again."

When the conversation changed to a new topic, the girls moved quietly away. They returned to the entrance gate of the park and sauntered in boldly. They intended to accost Mitza and see how he would act.

The two men were so engrossed in their conversation that they did not observe the girls until they were directly opposite the bench on which they were sitting. Nancy pretended to be surprised at seeing Mitza once more although she was highly amused to note the fellow's dismay.

"Why, how fortunate that we should meet again," she said, smiling disarmingly.

"If you're still after Miss Morse's address," the man cut in curtly, "I can't give it to you. I haven't seen the old lady since I reached Sea Cliff."

Nancy knew this to be a deliberate falsehood, but before she could decide just what tack to take next, Togo solved the problem for her. He made a sudden playful dart at Mitza. Thinking that the dog intended to bite him, the fellow sprang backward, and in his fright allowed a letter to drop from his hand.

Mitza kicked savagely at Togo and stooped to pick up the communication, but Nancy was too quick for him. She retrieved the missive first and did not hesitate to glance at it. In the upper left-hand corner a name and address stood out in bold writing. It read:

"Miss Fanny Morse, Box 14, Sea Cliff."

·14· *Help from Togo*

"GIVE me that letter!" Joe Mitza cried furiously.

With a scornful smile Nancy extended it for him to take, but as the man reached out his hand, a strong gust of wind carried the envelope away. Togo took up the pursuit, pounced upon the note, and began to tear at it with his sharp teeth.

"Confound that mutt!" Mitza exclaimed angrily.

Snatching up a heavy stick he beat the dog until Togo dropped the letter. Yelping with pain, the animal tried to run away, but the man held him by the collar and whipped him cruelly.

"Stop that!" Nancy ordered, darting forward. "Don't you dare strike my dog!"

She caught Mitza by the arm and pulled the fellow away from Togo. He pushed her roughly aside. George and Bess joined the fray and the three girls managed to rescue the dog, but not before he had bitten Mitza's finger a little.

"That beast ought to be shot!" the man shouted furiously. "He ruined my letter and now look what he's done to my hand!"

"You brought it upon yourself, I am afraid," Nancy replied coldly.

By this time many persons, attracted by Togo's yelps of pain, had gathered at the scene. Mitza was regarded unsympathetically by all who had witnessed the affair.

"Where's my letter?" he demanded, looking about him.

In the mêlée it had been torn into several pieces and trampled into the dirt. The wind had carried the bits of paper in every direction.

"I guess there's nothing left of it," Bess said shortly.

Nancy had seen two of the scattered bits of paper lodge in a tiny evergreen tree near by, but she did not reveal the fact. She meant to retrieve them herself after Mitza had gone.

"I ought to call in the police," the man blustered. "Destroying a valuable letter——"

"Why don't you notify the local officers?" Nancy challenged. "I think it would be a good idea."

Mitza gave the girl a sharp glance. Then he quickly went off, nursing his injured hand and muttering to himself.

"It served him right to be bitten," said a woman who had witnessed the affair. "He had no excuse to abuse the dog. That man is a scrounger and as worthless as a fellow could be."

"Do you know him?" Nancy inquired alertly.

"Decidedly. He owes me a bill of nearly ten dollars, and all for food. I run the Florence Restaurant here at the park."

"Has Mitza been eating without paying?"

"Yes. He orders everything on the menu and then pretends he'll pay for it the next day. He claimed his wealthy father was sending him a cheque, but that it had been delayed."

"Delayed permanently, I imagine," Nancy commented dryly.

"I guess I'll go after him right now and threaten to turn him over to the police," the woman announced. "I'll not let him cheat me."

She was moving away when Nancy remembered to ask if anyone answering Miss Morse's description ever took her meals at the Florence Restaurant.

"I don't recall such a person. We have a great many customers in a day," the woman replied regretfully, "and I'd hardly remember anyone unless he was outstanding in some way."

After the restaurant owner had gone and the crowd had melted away, Nancy went to the little evergreen tree and searched for the pieces torn from Joe Mitza's letter.

"I'm almost positive the note was from Miss Morse," she told her chums. "Her box number was on the envelope, but I can't be sure of it now."

"Here's one of the pieces!" Bess cried out triumphantly, picking it up from the ground. "It seems to be a part of the envelope."

Luck favoured the girls. Although the scrap of paper was only a tiny one, it bore the notation "Box 14."

"Now I'll be able to get in touch with Miss Morse!" Nancy declared, highly elated.

The girls searched for some minutes in the vicinity and finally discovered another portion of the letter which had blown into a flower bed.

"What does it say?" George demanded eagerly, peering over Nancy's shoulder.

" 'I'll come at night with the $5000,' " Nancy read aloud. "Oh, dear, this seems to indicate that the old lady intends to go through with some sort of deal with Mitza."

"Where are they to meet, do you suppose?" Bess speculated. "If only we had seen all of the letter!"

"Let's try to find a few more scraps," Nancy suggested. "Perhaps we'll be able to piece the thing together."

Although the girls searched diligently, they were unable to locate other portions of the letter. As they were looking under the porch of a tourist cabin, an elderly man with a cane came walking slowly down the cinder path. He paused to watch the girls curiously.

"Did you lose anything?" he inquired in a friendly tone.

"Only a piece of paper," Nancy replied, straightening up to gaze at the old gentleman.

He was an interesting type, agile and active despite his age, which one might guess to be about seventy.

"Could this be what you were looking for?" The old man pointed his cane towards a scrap of soiled wrapping paper lying on the ground.

"I'm afraid not," Nancy answered, returning his warm smile.

The old man sat down on a bench near by. Very shortly he introduced himself as a Mr Albin, and struck up a friendly conversation, revealing to his young listeners that his father originally had owned all the ground upon which the town of Sea Cliff stood.

"Until ten years ago this park was a part of my farm," he declared reminiscently. "I like to walk down here on sunny days, sort of thinking back on the good old times. I guess probably you've heard of the Albins. My ancestors settled here way back in 1712 and there's been an Albin in Sea Cliff ever since."

"You must know nearly everyone here, then," Nancy

commented thoughtfully. She had had an idea.

"There was a time when I did, but not any more. Sea Cliff has grown too fast for me in the past few years. But I know all the old-timers."

"Did you ever hear of the Conger family?" Nancy inquired.

"Fred Conger was one of my best friends. Why, the last few years of his life, he used to come to my house nearly every day and we would work on ship models together. Fred made one of an old fashioned brig, which was the neatest piece of work I ever saw. It took over a year to make it. He said that when it should be finished I should have it. But he didn't live long enough to fulfil his promise."

"Where is the ship now?"

"In the old Conger homestead, decaying with the rest of the furnishings. A great pity, too, for Conger loved beautiful things and believed in taking care of them. I'm partly responsible for the way matters turned out—I blame myself."

Nancy gazed at the old gentleman in astonishment.

"You are to blame, Mr Albin?" the Drew girl asked.

"Yes," the old man sighed. "I knew how Fred loved his daughter Bernice. In trying to soften the blow of her elopement I made a sad botch of things."

"I don't understand," Nancy murmured.

Mr Albin hesitated, and the girls sensed that it was a painful ordeal for him to tell them more. But he said quietly:

"You see, Fred kept hoping in the last years of his life that he would get some word from his daughter. He felt certain that she would write and tell him she was returning home. He talked almost constantly of her.

I don't know actually what became of the girl, but she caused her poor father untold grief.

"After a while I couldn't stand it to see Fred suffer as he did. It was a bit dishonest of me, I know, but a few years before his death I arranged to have postcards sent from various European ports, all of them signed 'Love, Bernice.' "

"And Mr Conger believed they came from his daughter?" Bess asked softly.

"Yes. Whenever he received a card he would be happy for days."

"Why, everything considered, I think that was a very kind thing for you to do," George remarked.

The old man shook his head. "I thought so too at first, but after Fred died I learned that he had left all his property in trust to his daughter, confidently believing her to be alive. The bank cannot close up the estate until she is found, and in the meantime the grand old place is falling into ruin."

"You believe Bernice Conger is dead?" Nancy asked thoughtfully.

"I don't know," the old man answered slowly. "But if she is still alive I'm afraid she'll never return here. Oh, it's a pity to see that fine old estate in such wretched condition. A pity!"

"You shouldn't blame yourself," Nancy said kindly. "You thought you were acting for the best."

"I didn't mean to do wrong, it's true, but that doesn't excuse me. Oh, I worry about it day and night."

"Does anyone here in Sea Cliff know about the postcards?" George questioned.

The old man looked startled.

·15· *A Page from the Past*

HE glanced nervously at the girls, and they noticed a stray tear trickling down his furrowed cheek.

"No, today is the first time I ever told anyone. I shouldn't have talked so much—promise you'll never repeat the story," he pleaded.

"Have no fear, we'll certainly guard your secret," Nancy answered sympathetically.

"Oh, thank you, thank you," the old man murmured gratefully and without a word of farewell he rose and moved slowly away.

Returning to the Seaside Hotel, Nancy and her chums were greeted in the foyer by Mr Drew. George and Bess went directly to their room. After they had gone, the lawyer took his daughter aside for a quiet talk.

"I have news of the seaplane pilot, Nancy. I spent nearly an hour at the hospital today talking with the doctors as well as the patient."

"Then the man has recovered consciousness?" Nancy asked eagerly.

"Yes. When I saw him he seemed little the worse for what he went through. Apparently you were right about the fellow having been drugged. The doctors feel certain of it, and I learned from the aviator that shortly before he took off in the seaplane a stranger accosted him. They struck up a friendly conversation, and the man treated him to a lunch with coffee."

"Dropping a few pills into the coffee, I suppose," said Nancy.

"So it would seem. While it is impossible to gain absolute evidence, I am convinced that Wormrath is at the bottom of the matter."

"Have you told Mr Owen what you learned?"

"Not yet. The nurse said he wasn't feeling as well as he was at first—shock, I suppose. If you have a few minutes to spare, Nancy, you might run up to his room."

"I'll be glad to, Dad," she promised, "just as soon as I've written a letter."

Nancy then told her father of her experience at the tourist park, and the manner in which she had gained Miss Morse's address.

"I intend to write to her immediately," she declared, "but I'm afraid even now it may be too late. From the bit of letter I found I gather she intends to hand over the five thousand dollars to Mitza very shortly."

Carson Drew nodded, scarcely heeding what his daughter was saying, for his mind was firmly fixed upon the Owen-Wormrath case. Nancy had intended to seek his advice, but realizing that he did not wish to be bothered just then, she said no more. Instead, she wrote a brief note to Miss Morse in which she told the woman of the suitcase still being at the hotel, and warning her to beware of Mitza.

"I've done practically all I can now," she thought as she dropped the letter into the mailbox. "I only hope it reaches Miss Morse in time to prevent her from acting rashly."

Feeling that an important duty had been accomplished, Nancy next called at Mr Owen's room and was admitted by the nurse.

"How is the patient?" the girl inquired in a low tone.

"He is sleeping just now," the nurse replied, leading Nancy to the bedside. "He had a temporary relapse about three hours ago, but his sleep is natural now. When he awakens I believe he will be very nearly back to normal."

Nancy sat down by the bed while the nurse lay down on a bed near by.

"Perhaps you would like to take a little walk out in the sunshine," Nancy presently suggested. "Mr Owen is sleeping and I don't mind staying with him."

The young woman thanked Nancy for her kindness, saying that she would enjoy a breath of fresh air.

"I'll not be gone more than fifteen minutes," she promised, closing the door softly as she went out.

Nancy picked up a magazine and started to read, but scarcely had she turned the first page when Mr Owen's eyelids opened. He gazed blankly about the room for a moment, then smiled at the girl.

"How do you feel, Mr Owen?" she asked.

"Oh, much better, much better," the man replied. "I feel as if I could eat a big meal. Do you suppose you could smuggle in a 'T' bone steak for me with French fried potatoes and a pot of coffee?"

"I'm afraid I couldn't until the nurse returns and says it will be all right," Nancy smiled. "You mustn't tire yourself by talking, either, Mr Owen."

"Nonsense! There's no sense in trying to make an invalid of me. Well, if I'm ordered not to talk, then you must do it for me!"

"I might tell you about my dog Togo," the girl

laughed, probing her mind for a topic which would amuse the man.

She related the terrier's many mischievous little tricks and revealed how the dog had come into her possession. At first Nancy did not mention Mrs Owen's name, although she longed to do so. But she feared that the patient might become excited. However, she was curious to learn if the clubwoman were related to Mr Owen, and finally broached the subject.

"Oh, yes, I must tell you about a curious coincidence," she said casually, watching the man closely. "The woman whose bag Togo dropped in the lake had your surname."

"Owen?" The man asked in surprise.

"Yes. I don't suppose you're related to anyone in my state, are you?"

"Well, not to my knowledge. The truth is, I have very few relatives anywhere. I'm practically alone in the world."

Mr Owen lapsed into moody silence, gazing meditatively out of the window. Nancy realized that unwittingly she had reminded him of an unhappy phase of his life, and wished that she had refrained from broaching the subject.

"My wife died many years ago," Mr Owen murmured, speaking as if to himself. "At that time I was travelling in Borneo. I had gone into the interior and did not even know that she was ill. I did not reach this country until several months after her death."

"A sad homecoming," Nancy said sympathetically.

"Shortly after reaching the United States I was stricken with a fever," Mr Owen continued. "I spent six months in a hospital. When I finally reached

Chicago, broken in health and hopelessly discouraged, I found our former home occupied by another family. No one could tell me where my wife had been buried."

"Had you no friends in the city?"

"None. We had lived there only a month, when I left for Borneo. After what happened I could not bear to remain in Chicago. I went to Windham, and after years of struggle began to prosper in the silk and woollen business. I suppose I am a successful man now, but my life is empty and desolate. I'd give everything to see Alice just once again."

"Alice?" Nancy inquired quickly. "Was that the name of your wife?"

"Yes, Alice Lenore. She was a very handsome woman."

"I was just thinking," Nancy murmured before she stopped to consider the effect her words might produce, "that the Mrs Owen of my acquaintance easily could be named Alice, too."

"What was that?" Mr Owen demanded sharply. He grasped Nancy's wrist, the fingers pressing into her flesh so hard that it hurt her.

"I don't really know Mrs Owen's first name," Nancy assured him quickly. "But I did chance to see a newspaper clipping which she kept in her handbag. It read: 'Rexy, come home. All is forgiven. Alice.' "

A strange light suddenly came into the patient's eyes and a bright flush crept over his pallid cheeks. He still gripped Nancy's wrist.

"You are sure?" he rasped, fairly beside himself with subdued excitement. "Those were the exact words?"

"Why yes, I'm almost certain of it, Mr Owen. Did you ever know anyone named Rexy?"

"Rexy was my nickname. But I can't understand it—my wife is dead. She couldn't have inserted the advertisement in the paper, and yet the names—Rexy and Alice—tell me, is Mrs Owen a woman of middle age?"

"I should judge her to be around sixty."

"Alice was only two years younger than myself and I am sixty-two now," Mr Owen murmured. "Tell me, is your friend a handsome woman?"

"I should consider her so," Nancy answered, and described Mrs Owen as best she could.

"She *is* my wife, my Alice!" Mr Owen cried, throwing aside the bed covers. "There has been some terrible mistake. She must be alive, and I am going to her!"

It required all of Nancy's strength to keep Mr Owen in bed. He struggled and tried to resist her as she placed the covers over him.

"Don't try to keep me away from my wife! We've been separated so many years. I must go to her!"

"You're in no condition to travel now," Nancy insisted. "Wouldn't it be much better to send a telegram to Mrs Owen and find out if she really is your wife?"

"Yes, yes, send her a telegram at once," Mr Owen urged. "Bring me paper and pencil and I'll write it now."

Nancy was sorry that she had broached the subject of the newspaper clipping. While she was elated over the relationship which appeared to exist between the two persons, she realized that Mr Owen was too excited for his own good. She feared that he might have a relapse, particularly if it should develop that the clubwoman was not his wife after all.

"It doesn't seem possible that my Alice may still be alive," the man mumbled as he scribbled a few lines on the paper Nancy handed him. "And yet her death was never confirmed. Oh, I don't dare hope for such luck."

"We'll soon know the truth," Nancy replied soothingly. "Until then you must be calm and be prepared for a possible disappointment."

"Will you send the telegram right away?" Mr Owen pleaded.

"Yes, this very instant."

Nancy telephoned the local telegraph office, repeating the message as Mr Owen had written it.

"How long will it take before we can receive a reply?" the man asked nervously.

"Oh, several hours at least. You must try to rest, Mr Owen."

"I can't rest until I know the truth. Oh, if only I dared hope——"

The patient began to roll and toss on the bed, throwing his head about restlessly. Once he tried to get up, and Nancy had to restrain him forcibly.

"I wish the nurse would return," she said to herself anxiously.

Even to the girl's untrained eye it was evident that the man had taken a turn for the worse. Her conscience troubled her, for she realized that she had been the cause of the relapse.

"I didn't intend to excite him," she comforted herself. "I only wanted to help him."

Just then the door opened and the nurse entered. Without removing her hat she rushed to the bedside.

"What have you done to him?" she demanded angrily of Nancy.

"Nothing," the girl murmured contritely. "We talked and——"

"You've excited him, that's what you've done. Oh, I shouldn't have left him for a minute! Call a doctor at once, then go away and don't allow anyone to enter this room!"

It was a new experience for Nancy to be ordered about, but she accepted the reprimand meekly. She flew to the telephone, and not knowing the name of a local doctor she asked the house physician to come upstairs immediately.

"I shouldn't have spoken so harshly," the nurse apologized. "I'm sure it wasn't your fault——"

"But it was," Nancy replied, accepting full responsibility. "I'll go away now."

She slipped out into the hall, and was standing just outside the door as her father came down the carpeted corridor.

"How is Mr Owen?" he inquired cheerfully, and was startled to glimpse Nancy's downcast face. "He's not worse?"

"Yes, he is, Dad, and I'm the cause of it, too. Oh, I'm so sorry about it."

After listening to her account of the conversation with the sick man, Mr Drew did not spare his daughter's feelings.

"It was a very foolish thing to do, Nancy. In the first place, you're far from certain that Mrs Owen is my client's wife. Such a supposition sounds a bit preposterous to me."

"But everything tallies," Nancy protested, moving to defend herself. "Mr Owen's nickname is Rexy, and his wife's name was Alice——"

"Even so, you should have known better. Alice Owen is a fairly common name. You've led Mr Owen to hope that his wife may be alive. Now, if he learns it is all a mistake I shudder to think of the result."

"You mean—he might die?" Nancy gasped, completely shaken. "I didn't realize he was so ill. He seemed strong and cheerful."

"Mr Owen has a powerful will," Carson Drew replied grimly, "but he has a weak heart. You meant well, Nancy, but this time I'm afraid that in your great zeal to solve mysteries you have overstepped yourself."

"What can I do, Dad?" the girl asked unhappily.

"There is nothing anyone can do," her father returned gravely. "We must wait for the reply to your telegram, and hope that the news will be favourable."

·16·   Nancy's "Mistake"

IN a few minutes the doctor arrived and immediately was admitted to Mr Owen's room. Nancy hovered nervously in the hallway.

Nearly half an hour elapsed before the physician emerged. When the girl observed his grave face it required all her courage to ask him about the patient's condition.

"Mr Owen has been greatly over-stimulated," the doctor replied, "and his heart is weak. But if he suffers no further shock I look for an improvement within a day or two."

Nancy went away meekly to find Bess and George.

"Oh, I feel dreadful about what I did," she confided after she had told them about everything. "Everyone blames me for Mr Owen's relapse, and I deserve it. I was so eager to prove the relationship between the couple that I didn't consider the effect my words might have upon Mr Owen, should my theory prove false."

"But if you're right, Nancy, the reunion will be wonderful," Bess said kindly.

"Yes, but it's almost too much to expect—that Mrs Owen could be the missing wife of my father's client. Mr Owen is certain she died years ago. It doesn't seem as if there could be a mistake—and yet, I keep hoping."

"Try not to think any more about it until the telegram comes," George urged, for she saw that Nancy was greatly upset with worry. "You acted with the best of intentions, and I'm sure no one suspected that Mr Owen was in such a nervous condition."

"Results are all that count—not good intentions," Nancy said gloomily. "If Mr Owen should die, I'll be responsible——"

"Oh, now you're getting morbid," Bess cut in. "Mr Owen won't die."

"He might," Nancy insisted. "If the telegram is unfavourable it wouldn't surprise me a bit if he should."

"I'm sure it's not that serious," George said cheerfully. "Don't worry, Nancy, and tell me what you're wearing to the dance tonight."

"Dance?"

"You've not forgotten?" Bess questioned in astonishment. "We promised Jack we'd go to the party this evening at the Country Club."

"Oh, I did forget! I can't go now."

"But it's a dinner dance," Bess reminded her. "Our

reservations are made. It isn't really fair to Jack to refuse now."

"I suppose I'll have to go since I promised," Nancy consented reluctantly, "but with Mr Owen so ill it doesn't seem right."

When Jack called for the girls later that evening, he sensed immediately that something was amiss. He too, became downcast when he learned of Mr Owen's condition.

Everyone tried to be cheerful and enter into the spirit of the festivities, but the entertainment had lost its zest for them all. The dinner which preceded it was excellent, yet Nancy made only a pretence of eating. Later in the ballroom she danced mechanically, and more than once was compelled to apologize because she had failed to follow an intricate step.

"I don't know what the matter is with me," she said to Jack as she danced with him. "I'm ruining your entire evening."

"You're worried, Nancy, and I don't blame you a bit. This isn't much of a party anyway. What do you say we leave and go for a spin in my car? The other girls won't mind. They're having a good time."

"I'd love it, Jack. A little fresh air may clear my mind."

It was delightful to motor swiftly over the paved road, the breeze blowing against their faces. Finally Nancy observed:

"Isn't this the road which leads to Old Estate?"

"Yes," her companion nodded. "We're almost at the Conger place now. At the crest of the next knoll you'll see the grounds."

"Everything looks different at night."

The car moved over the tiny hill, and Nancy gazed in the direction Jack indicated.

"Would you like to stop and take another look at the Whispering Statue?" he inquired.

"Oh, not tonight, Jack. We must be getting back to the clubhouse soon. But are you certain that is the Conger estate?"

"Why, of course, Nancy. You're not accustomed to the way it looks at night, but I know this road like a veteran bus driver."

"There's a light over there where you pointed," Nancy insisted. "The Conger estate is deserted."

Jack slowed down the car so that he might glance more carefully towards the grounds which were shrouded behind a pine grove.

"There's no light, Nancy. But it's the Conger estate. I've passed it dozens of times."

"I'm certain I saw a light. It's gone now."

Young Kingdon brought the automobile to a halt by the roadside not far from the private entrance to the grounds.

"Where did you see it?" he questioned.

"Why, in the trees, apparently from the old house. The light flashed three times."

"You're certain you saw it, Nancy?"

"Yes, indeed, I believe it was a signal."

"I can't imagine who would be prowling about the place at this time of night," Jack said thoughtfully. "I guess I'll walk up there and look round."

"I'll go with you."

"No, stay in the car," Jack replied. "I might run into trouble. If I don't return in ten minutes come after me, or go for help."

Nancy did not like such an arrangement. She greatly preferred to do her own investigating, but the young man had very decided ideas about gallantry and would not allow her to accompany him. While Nancy sat waiting in the car, she tried to figure out what the strange light might signify.

"It's barely possible Mr Albin is in the house trying to recover the ship model which old Mr Conger promised him," she reflected. "Yet that scarcely seems plausible either, for he wouldn't go prowling into houses at night."

The ten minutes elapsed, and Nancy opened the car door, determined to go in search of Jack. There was no need for her to do so, however. Just then the young man came down the private driveway, whistling a gay tune.

"False alarm," he called out cheerfully.

"Was there no light?" Nancy asked in disappointment.

"No, the place is as quiet as a tomb. The only sound comes from the sea."

"I'm certain I saw a light," Nancy murmured. "I'm positive it flashed three times."

"Imagination plays tricks upon us all now and then," her companion laughed.

He turned the car round in the road and drove back towards the clubhouse. Nancy was very quiet. She could not believe that her imagination had tricked her, yet she did not wish to contradict her escort, either.

"I believe someone must have been skulking about the grounds," she thought. "Whoever the person was, he probably extinguished his light before Jack could see the house."

At the country club, Nancy danced several numbers,

then was relieved when Bess and George suggested that they all go back to the hotel. The girls were tired, and without meaning to do so, slept late the next morning. Just after nine o'clock Nancy's telephone rang.

"A telegram for you," said the voice of the hotel clerk. "We'll send it right up."

The girl whirled round to face Bess and George.

"Of course, the wire is from Mrs Owen! Oh, I'm almost afraid to read it."

Nancy had the door open before the bell boy could knock. With the yellow envelope in her hand she leaned weakly against the wall.

"Oh, open it and find out what it says," Bess urged.

"Here, let me do it," George offered, taking the message from her chum. She ripped open the envelope. "Yes, it's from Mrs Owen, all right."

Nancy could not bear the suspense.

"Let me see it," she cried, and reclaimed the sheet of paper. Her face was a study as she read the message.

"What does she say?" Bess asked eagerly. "Was your theory right, Nancy?"

"Yes, it was! I don't understand why anyone thought Mrs Owen wasn't living."

"Of course she is living," George chuckled. "We knew that before we left River Heights!"

"You don't understand what I mean. The woman we met in the park is Alice Owen, the wife of my father's client! She's overwhelmed to learn that her husband still lives, so she must have thought he was dead. She is ready to start for Sea Cliff at once if Mr Owen still wishes to see her after all these years."

"If he wishes to see her!" Bess echoed. "The poor man will be overjoyed."

"Yes," Nancy agreed, "but I don't intend to make the same mistake twice. Mr Owen must be prepared properly for the good news so that he'll not become excited again. I'll entrust the message to the nurse and let her give it to him when she thinks the time advisable to do so."

Highly elated, and feeling that in a way she had redeemed herself, Nancy took the telegram to the man's room where she quietly inquired about the condition of the patient.

"He is much better today," the nurse replied. "However, he worries constantly. It really will help him to know about his wife, for he'll have no peace of mind until he does."

Nancy was relieved to hear this opinion, and felt happy that she could report the good news which was in store for the patient. She left the message with the young woman, who promised to read it to Mr Owen when he became a trifle stronger.

That afternoon, the man was told of the contents of the telegram from his wife. It was impossible for him not to become somewhat excited, but he accepted the news as quietly as possible. Tears of joy trickled down his cheeks.

"Tell Alice I do want her," he murmured. "Make her understand that I need her more than ever—that it was all a horrible mistake, our separation. If only I might talk with her just for a moment!"

When Nancy heard this, it occurred to her that Mr Owen easily might convey his own message by means of a long distance telephone call. Yet, having learned one lesson, she thought it best not to utter this thought. Instead, she quietly consulted the doctor.

"Why yes, I believe Mr Owen is strong enough now to withstand the excitement," the physician agreed after a moment's reflection. "However, the conversation must be brief."

Nancy was happy to put the call through, and after warning Mrs Owen that she must speak only a few words, she handed the instrument over to the trembling patient.

"Alice," he gasped, scarcely above a whisper, "is it really you?"

The listeners in the room could not hear the reply, but a happy light shone upon Mr Owen's face as he recognized the familiar voice of his wife. He murmured a few loving words; then the nurse stepped forward and gently took the phone from his hand.

"Just a minute longer," he pleaded, but she firmly shook her head.

"You will see your wife soon," Nancy said to reconcile him.

"Tomorrow," he murmured happily as he dropped wearily back against the pillows. "She is coming on the first train she can get."

The nurse sent everyone from the room so that the patient might sleep. In the corridor Carson Drew smiled at his daughter.

"I'm sorry I reprimanded you yesterday, Nancy," he apologized. "After all, everything has turned out extremely well. Mr and Mrs Owen will be eternally grateful to you."

"And I'll always be grateful to Mr Owen for postponing his dying day," Nancy laughed. "I feel as if a ten-ton weight had been lifted from my shoulders."

"So do I," Mr Drew admitted. He removed a five-dollar bill from his wallet. "Here, you deserve a celebration, Nancy. Take this and buy yourself a good time."

"I'll buy myself a white bathing suit instead," Nancy said. "They're all the fashion here at Sea Cliff. Thanks, Dad."

Bess and George were eager to do some shopping too, for they wished to purchase gifts to take home to some young cousins. They were delighted to accompany Nancy to the business district of Sea Cliff and help her select the new swim suit.

It was after six o'clock when the girls returned to the hotel. Fearing that Mr Drew would be annoyed because they would delay dinner, they hurried towards the elevator. Nancy did not stop to ask if there was any mail. She was surprised when the hotel clerk signalled to her.

"This letter came late this afternoon, special delivery. I thought it might be important."

Nancy thanked him and took the communication, noticing that it was stamped Sea Cliff. At first she thought it might be from Jack, but she immediately abandoned that idea when she saw that the address had been written by a woman.

Opening the letter, she glanced at the bottom of the page to learn the identity of the writer. Then, her eyes sparkling with excitement, she moved swiftly towards her chums.

"Girls," she announced in delight, "at last I've heard from Miss Morse!"

· 17 ·   *A Happy Reunion*

NANCY eagerly scanned the note from Miss Morse, and as she did so her face reflected disappointment.

"What does she have to say?" Bess inquired curiously.

"We're to leave the suitcase at the railway station luggage office and tell the attendant that Miss Morse will call for it later," Nancy replied, her eyes still upon the page.

"And doesn't she give her own address?" George questioned.

Nancy carefully inspected both the letter and the envelope. The message had been written upon the cheapest type of paper.

"No, I think she omitted it on purpose. Then too, she ignored what I wrote about Joe Mitza. I thought Miss Morse would tell me to bring the suitcase to wherever she is staying. That way I could reveal all I know about that trickster who is after her money."

"You'd get no thanks for it," Bess replied. "Miss Morse is a most ungrateful sort of person."

"What will you do about the suitcase, Nancy?" inquired George.

"Oh, take it to the station, I suppose. It will be no bother, for we can leave it there when we go to meet Mrs Owen."

Having received word as to which train the club-woman would arrive upon, the girls taxied to the station early the next morning. After depositing Miss Morse's bag with the luggage attendant, they waited at the passenger gate.

The train was on time, and in a few minutes they caught sight of Mrs Owen, followed by a porter, coming towards them eagerly. She greeted the girls cordially, and squeezed Nancy's hand as she tried to thank her for everything the girl had done.

"Even now I can scarcely believe that the good news is true," she murmured, tears of joy welling in her eyes. "I thought my husband disappeared in Borneo years ago. Tell me, how is Charles? Is he past all danger?"

"Yes, providing he does not become too excited," Nancy answered. "The doctor thinks it may be several days before he'll be able to leave his bed."

"And may I see him at once," Mrs Owen pleaded, "or must I wait until he is stronger?"

"The doctor said you might talk with him for a few minutes," Nancy smiled, steering the woman towards a waiting taxi. "I am certain your husband could not bear it if anyone tried to keep you away from him for even an hour longer."

Nancy and her chums did not witness the happy reunion which took place at the hotel, for only the nurse was in the sickroom when Mrs Owen entered it. The girls waited in the corridor. Fifteen minutes later the clubwoman emerged, her face radiant.

"Oh, Nancy," she murmured, clasping the girl's hand. "It's too wonderful. It seems almost like a dream. To think that all these many years my husband and I have believed each other dead! Had it not been for you our lives would have continued bleak and empty."

"You really owe everything to the dog Togo," Nancy smiled. "If he hadn't scampered away with your bag I'd never have met you at all."

"I must do something very handsome for that little fellow," Mrs Owen declared. "I'll buy him a fine new leather harness."

"I hope he'll wear it," Nancy said. "Togo has very pronounced likes and dislikes, and hates any kind of restrictions."

With Mrs Owen comfortably established in a suite adjoining the room of her husband, Nancy and her chums sought out Mr Trixler. They drove the elderly man to the Brighton Baths and went for a swim themselves. Late in the afternoon when they were back at the hotel and time was heavy on the girls' hands, Nancy had a proposal to offer.

"Let's borrow Mr Trixler's car and drive out to Old Estate," she said.

"We've seen all there is out at that place," George protested. "It certainly seems somehow to fascinate you, Nancy."

"It does, I'll admit. But I have a special reason for wishing to go at this time."

"To see if the 'Whispering Girl' is still there?" Bess asked teasingly.

"That's it exactly," Nancy replied soberly. "I have reason to think it might be gone. When Jack and I passed the place I saw a light moving among the trees. Jack investigated, but could find no one there, so he was inclined to think it was all my imagination, but I know better. Someone was prowling about the grounds, I'm sure."

"Perhaps that contractor went back to steal the marble statue," George said quickly. "He seemed to want it very badly."

"I thought of that possibility," Nancy admitted. "Or it could have been Mr Albin searching for the ship model."

"I don't believe that pleasant old man would enter the house without permission," Bess declared. "I'd sooner think it was the contractor after the statue."

"Anyway, I'd like to drive out there and look round the place in daylight," Nancy went on. "Don't you want to come along?"

Learning that an adventure might be in store for them, George quickly changed her opinion about there being nothing more to see at Old Estate. Both she and Bess accepted their chum's invitation with alacrity.

Soon the car reached the private road leading to the untenanted estate. As the girls drove towards the abandoned house, they noticed no fresh automobile tyre tracks along the way. Nancy stopped the car under an oak tree. Alighting, she walked up and down the road for some distance to examine the ground carefully.

"No truck has passed through here in the past three days," she told her chums. "That cancels our theory about the contractor trying to haul away the marble statues."

They drove on to the house, and Nancy parked the car in a clump of bushes. A casual glance did not reveal anything amiss. The Whispering Girl remained undisturbed, and in trying the door handles of the decaying dwelling, she found everything securely locked—the same as upon their former visit.

"I guess perhaps Jack was right after all," George

teased her chum. "You must have imagined you saw those lights, Nancy."

The girl offered no reply. She knew she had not been mistaken. However, she was puzzled to find no evidence of the prowler.

The girls sat down by the fountain and listened to the angry roar of the ocean.

"This place gives me the creeps," Bess shivered. "I don't see why you like to come here, Nancy."

"Ever since we arrived in Sea Cliff, our detective chum has been trying to tack a mystery on to this place," George chuckled. "The setting is perfect, but somehow the mystery refuses to develop."

Nancy suddenly held up her hand in a gesture which commanded silence.

"Ssh! Someone is coming up the road!"

Bess and George sprang to their feet thoroughly alarmed. They too heard the dry crackling sound of someone shuffling through the thick bed of leaves which covered the rutty road.

"Let's get away from here," Bess gasped.

Catching George by the hand, she pulled her cousin into the woods. Nancy did not follow her chums. Instead, she stepped quickly behind the Whispering Girl statue. The Drew girl wore a close fitting white silk dress which tended to blend in with the marble figure. She trusted that in the gathering dusk she would not be observed unless she chose to make her presence known.

Nancy fully expected to see either the contractor or Mr Albin. When instead a bent old woman plodded into view, she was greatly surprised. She became astounded when she recognized the person as Miss Fanny Morse.

·18· A Rendezvous

NANCY crouched behind the Whispering Girl statue, wondering what had brought Miss Morse to the Conger estate. The old lady carried the suitcase which the girls had left earlier in the day at the railway station luggage office. She appeared very tired as if she had walked from Sea Cliff. While still some distance from the garden, she set the bag down and leaned wearily against a tree trunk.

"She's here to meet someone," Nancy reasoned as she saw the old woman glance at her watch. "I wonder if it can be Mitza."

After a few minutes Miss Morse rose. Picking up the bag, she trudged on towards the house and glanced casually towards the statue, then looked away.

The mysterious person walked round to a side door, and for a moment was out of view. Nancy daringly emerged from her hiding place to look on.

The side door stood slightly ajar. Miss Morse evidently had entered the house.

"How did she get in?" Nancy speculated. "That door was locked. She must have a key."

The girl was debating whether or not to follow the woman inside, when she heard footsteps. Someone was coming up the road.

Just in time, Nancy darted back behind the group of statues. Joe Mitza came walking up hurriedly, as if late for an appointment.

"I was right!" Nancy thought triumphantly. "I've either interrupted an important rendezvous or am about to witness one!"

The girl had no intention of letting Miss Morse become the innocent victim of Mitza's fraudulent scheme, and would do all she could to prevent it. If only she might go after the police! She knew there was not time for that. Before she would have a chance to return with the officers Mitza doubtless would have obtained the woman's five thousand dollars.

The man had paused not far from the garden. Nancy saw him remove a package of money from his pocket and count it hurriedly.

"He's here to meet Miss Morse, all right," she reflected. "Oh, I can't let him cheat her."

For an instant Nancy was tempted to step out and confront the trickster, but she suspected that should it come to an argument, she could not depend upon Miss Morse to stand by her, for the peculiar old lady seemed to be of a contrary disposition. She would probably side with Mitza.

"If I do save that five thousand dollars for her I'll have to do so in spite of Miss Morse, rather than with her help," she reflected.

Nancy was sorely puzzled as to what course to follow, when suddenly an idea came to her. She would frighten the man by whispering to him a warning which would appear to come from the marble statue!

Nancy realized that Mitza might investigate, in which case she would be discovered. It was worth trying.

"I'll be aided by the gathering darkness and the roar of the ocean," she thought. "The setting is almost perfect for the 'Whispering Girl' to speak."

Nancy wrapped her white dress closer about her so that the wind could not whip it into view. Then she began to moan softly, trying to blend the weird sound with the sighing of the wind in the pine boughs overhead.

Joe Mitza stood perfectly still and looked at the marble statue, listening intently.

"K-e-e-p a-w-a-y," Nancy whispered warningly. "K-e-e-p a-w-a-y."

Joe Mitza fingered the roll of bills nervously and Nancy knew that he had heard. She could see him straining his ears in an attempt to hear the statue speak again. His lips moved slightly as he muttered something to himself.

"He is not sure if he actually did hear the warning," she thought.

Nancy bided her time and waited until she saw that Mitza was convinced his ears had tricked him. With a shrug of his shoulders he turned towards the house.

"K-e-e-p a-w-a-y," Nancy whispered again in the same mournful tone. "K-e-e-p a-w-a-y."

This time Mitza knew that he had heard the voice. With a gasp of fear he turned and bolted down the road. The packet of money fell from his hands.

Nancy leaned weakly against the statue and laughed softly to herself. Quickly she smothered her merriment as a man's curt voice rang out through the trees:

"There he goes! After him, men!"

She heard a great crackling of the underbrush and saw several shadowy figures emerge from the shrubbery along the road as they took up pursuit after Joe Mitza.

"Police officers!" Nancy thought in astonishment. "They must have followed him to Old Estate and been lying in wait."

A stick broke sharply just behind Nancy. She sprang backwards, it startled her so, but she laughed in relief as she saw Bess and George.

"Oh, Nancy, come away quickly before we're seen," the latter pleaded. "This is no place for us. We've run into some sort of police ambush, I think, and we might be arrested as suspicious persons."

"Did you see a man running down the road?" Nancy asked.

"Yes, he acted as if he were frightened half out of his wits," Bess returned nervously, plucking at her chum's sleeve in an effort to pull her towards the sheltering woods. "George and I saw everything. A police car drove up and the officers hid along the shrubbery. Then this man came running down the private road and they started to chase him."

"He was Mitza," Nancy supplied. "I hope the police captured him."

"They didn't," George answered. "The fellow escaped into the woods."

"Do come away, Nancy," Bess insisted fearfully. "Listen to the wind howl! It sounds as if ghosts were talking, and I'm afraid."

"Silly," Nancy laughed. "No, I won't leave just yet. First I must find the roll of money Mitza dropped when I frightened him."

"What did you do?" said George.

"Oh, nothing much. I just whispered a warning from behind this statue."

"Some day you'll be a bit too daring," Bess said severely. "Please, let's leave."

"You may go if you wish, but I intend to find the money Mitza dropped when he fled."

Nancy began to grope about the place where the man had stood, but she could not see very plainly in the dark. Overhead black clouds were rolling menacingly. Rain might begin to fall at any minute. Bess and George helped in the search, and soon the latter found the roll of paper money which she gave to Nancy.

"There must be a fortune here!" George gasped. "What will you do with it, Nancy?"

"Oh, give it to the police, or else throw it away."

"Throw it away?" George echoed in a shocked tone.

"The money is worthless. I can tell by the feel of the paper that it's all fake stuff."

"Mitza must have intended to exchange it for Miss Morse's genuine money," Bess murmured. "You ruined his little game, Nancy."

"For the time being, but he may try the same trick later on. That's why I must go into the house and warn Miss Morse."

"You'd not enter that spooky old place now that it's so dark?" Bess asked incredulously. "Let's go back to the car, Nancy."

"You and George go. It will take me only a minute to talk to Miss Morse."

"The house is dreadfully quiet," Bess said. "I don't believe anyone is inside."

"You're just saying that," Nancy smiled. "Miss Morse must still be there, and I intend to talk with her."

Bess and George realized that their chum's mind was made up. They offered rather half-heartedly to accompany her if she insisted, but Nancy said that she preferred to go alone.

"Wait in the car for me," she told them. "I'll join you just as soon as I can."

"Please be careful, Nancy," George warned her friend as they turned away.

"There's no danger with Mitza gone," she replied carelessly. "Now try not to worry, for I promise you no big bad ghost will get me."

Smiling to herself, Nancy slipped the packet of money into her dress and moved swiftly towards the gloomy old mansion.

·19· *Strange Visitors*

QUIETLY Nancy went round to the side door which stood slightly ajar, and stood there listening in the shadow.

All was silent within, but from far down the beach the girl heard someone approaching the house from that direction.

Instantly Nancy thought that Joe Mitza, after escaping from the police, had circled the Conger grounds to keep his appointment with Miss Morse. She slipped out of sight round the corner of the house and waited.

Nancy heard shuffling steps, and at last glimpsed a bent figure which bore no resemblance to the tall, thin form of Mitza. In the darkness she could not see who was approaching.

The newcomer advanced towards the house very

slowly, almost timidly. He paused some distance from Nancy and stood looking nervously about the grounds.

"It is a dishonourable thing to do," she heard him mutter to himself. "How ashamed I'd be if anyone were to catch me."

"Why, it's Mr Albin!" the girl thought in relief, and without considering the startling effect she might have upon the old man, she stepped from her hiding place to confront him.

"Oh, my!" the old man cried in alarm.

"Don't be frightened," Nancy said in a low tone as she stooped to pick up the old gentleman's cane which had fallen from his hand. "Don't you remember me?"

"Are you a friend?" Mr Albin asked in a terrified quaver. "It's so dark I can't see you."

"I am Nancy Drew, the girl with whom you talked in the park. You were telling me about Mr Conger and his beautiful ship models."

"Oh, yes, yes, I remember," Mr Albin answered, greatly relieved. "You won't tell anyone you saw me here, will you?"

"No, of course not," Nancy assured the elderly man, steering him away from the house, for she was afraid their voices might reach the ears of Miss Morse. "But what brought you here, Mr Albin? You seem all worn out."

"I am pretty badly tuckered," the old gentleman admitted, sitting down wearily on the sagging veranda steps. "I've been tramping about all day long, trying to get up enough courage to come here and do a wicked deed."

"Do you intend to take the ship model which Mr Conger promised you?" Nancy smiled.

"Yes, but I hate a thief. I never stole anything in all my life. You believe me, don't you?"

"Why, of course, and I don't consider it stealing to take something which was given to you. The ship model really belongs to you."

"That's the way I figured it out," Mr Albin replied, obviously relieved that Nancy saw the matter as he did. "The piece is really my property and I can't bear to see it lost forever, especially when Mr Conger spent so many months working on it. This old homestead won't last a great deal longer."

The man pushed the head of his stout cane through the decaying wood of the veranda post to show that the outside covering of the building was only a hollow shell.

"Termites," he informed Nancy. "Main supports are in the same condition. One good storm, and the entire house will crash into the sea and float away."

"I should think the company that holds the estate in trust for Mr Conger's daughter would take the valuable furnishings from the house."

"That outfit will do nothing," Mr Albin replied scornfully. "Their sole interest in the place is to collect fat fees. I went to see the administrator yesterday to ask him if I might have the ship model. The man refused me permission to remove anything from the house."

"So you decided to come here anyway and take your rightful property?"

"Yes. I'd never have risked it, only the sky looks threatening. I'm afraid there is a bad storm brewing. If a hard blow should come, only a miracle would spare this mansion."

"I don't blame you a bit," Nancy said. "I think I'd do the same thing myself."

Old Mr Albin painfully rose from the steps. He glanced uneasily towards the homestead, shivering as he contemplated entering it.

"I'd hate to be seen doing this," he said.

Nancy thought that it was time she warned him about Miss Morse.

"If I were you I'd wait a little while before trying to get the ship model, Mr Albin. A strange woman is inside the house now."

"A woman? What is she doing here?"

"I'm sure I don't know. I wish I did."

"She must have come to steal some of the furnishings," the old man cried, excitedly. "Mr Conger collected valuable antiques, and it would be very easy for anyone to take them."

Thoroughly incensed at this thought, Mr Albin hobbled towards the front door. Before Nancy could prevent him, he had pounded on the heavy panels.

"I'll not let anyone—" he began angrily, then broke off suddenly to clutch wildly at the door knob for support.

He toppled sideways against the wall, gasping for breath. Quickly Nancy caught the aged man about the waist to keep him from falling.

"Are you ill, Mr Albin?" she asked in fright.

"My heart—I've had one of my attacks."

"You've exerted yourself too much," Nancy told him. "All this excitement and worry has been exhausting to you."

"I can't let that woman steal——"

"We'll go to town and inform the administrator of the estate about it," Nancy urged gently. "Come, I'll help you to the car."

Mr Albin let himself be led away from the house, leaning heavily upon Nancy, who was almost worn out when she came within view of the auto. Then George and Bess ran to assist her.

Before they reached Sea Cliff, the old man suffered another heart attack, making his breathing difficult. He did not object when Nancy said that she was taking him to a physician.

"Doctor Whimple will look after me," Mr Albin murmured. "He's done so for years."

Nancy found the Whimple residence, and there left Mr Albin under the care of the medical man. He assured the girls that he would keep the patient at his own home until he should have recovered fully from the illness.

On her way to Sea Cliff Nancy noticed that the car engine seemed to have developed a loud knock. As they drove away from the doctor's home it pounded so hard that Bess and George became aware of the sound, too.

"Goodness! What is wrong?" Bess asked with misgivings. "I hope we've not burned out a bearing."

"It's nothing like that," Nancy replied, "but I think we ought to see a garage mechanic. This is Mr Trixler's car and we can't afford to take any chances."

At the first garage the attendant was nowhere in sight. She tooted her horn impatiently.

"I'm in a hurry to get back to Old Estate," she fretted. "If I waste very much time here I'll not be able to see Miss Morse."

Nancy promptly backed her auto from the garage, intending to go elsewhere. As she reached the pavement, she suddenly applied her brakes, and looked intently at a truck which stood near a gasoline pump at the kerb. Evidently its driver was waiting for service, also.

"Girls," she exclaimed, "the driver is the contractor who owns the monkey!"

He appeared to be arguing with a passenger in the seat beside him. The two were talking as rapidly as possible, apparently bickering over the price of some commodity. The foreigner constantly lapsed into his native tongue, but Nancy gathered enough of the talk to suspect that the fellow was trying to sell the other man a marble statue.

"Surely he wouldn't dare attempt to steal the 'Whispering Girl,'" she thought. "It must be another piece that he means."

The argument was waxing warmer, with each man accusing the other of dishonesty. At length the contractor, losing all patience, muttered something about not waiting any longer for gas. Without glancing backwards he suddenly threw his car into reverse. The rear end hit the bumper of Nancy's car, striking it with such force that it gave the girls a rude jolt.

The man thrust his head from the car window. Nancy was certain that he recognized her. Instead of apologizing, however, he ducked hastily back behind the wheel and drove away rapidly.

· 20 · *At Work in the Dark*

NANCY and her chums sprang from the car to inspect the bumper. One side had been torn loose by the impact, so that it dragged upon the ground.

"Well, of all the ungrateful, contemptible tricks!" George exclaimed indignantly. "That's the way he treats us after rescuing his monkey."

"What will Mr Trixler say when he sees this?" Bess wailed. "He'll not let us have the car again."

"I don't want him to see it," Nancy answered grimly. "I'll have it repaired right now and pay for it myself if I must."

"That contractor should pay," George insisted. "Let's go to his home and collect."

"Tomorrow," Nancy promised. "Just now my chief aim is to get back to Old Estate. I hope it will not take long to have the car fixed up."

When the mechanic finally returned he assured them he would repair the bumper very cheaply, but shook his head as he listened to the knock in the engine.

"It's nothing serious, is it?" Nancy inquired anxiously. "May we have the car in a few minutes?"

The attendant smilingly shook his head. "It will take a good hour and a half, perhaps longer, to fix it."

"We might eat supper while we're waiting," Bess interposed hopefully.

"That restaurant across the street serves pretty fair food," the mechanic said.

"I'm half starved," George declared. "Come along, Nancy. Let's try it."

The auto was ready when the chums returned to the garage. Nancy paid the bill and soon was speeding towards Old Estate. She felt strangely elated, while her chums by contrast grew more gloomy and depressed as they approached the abandoned place. She parked the car out of sight along the main highway.

"You girls wait here until I see if Miss Morse is still at

the house," she advised. "No use in taking the automobile up the bumpy private road. It's too hard on the
tyres."

Bess and George offered a feeble protest, but really
welcomed the opportunity to remain behind.

"Hurry back," George warned her chum anxiously
as Nancy slipped away into the darkness. "It looks as if
it might storm soon."

As she walked swiftly up the road, the Drew girl
noticed deep wheel marks in the soft earth and was
inclined to believe they had been made since her last
visit to the estate. She approached the Conger house
cautiously. As she came within view of it she saw that a
truck had drawn up near the garden.

She halted in amazement. The contractor and the
same companion she had seen with him at the Sea Cliff
garage were placing one of the smaller marble statues
into the truck!

When the statue had been lowered safely into the
truck, the two men rested from their labours. But their
tongues did not remain idle. They talked excitedly, still
arguing over prices.

Nancy remained motionless in the shadow of an oak
tree, listening in astonishment. She gleaned that the
contractor was trying to drive a close bargain with the
other, selling him the three marble statues which he
professed to own.

"Why, he's deliberately stealing them from the
Conger estate," Nancy thought indignantly.

Boldly she stepped from behind the tree and walked
towards the men. They sprang apart when they saw her
coming. However, as the owner of the monkey recognized the girl, he eyed her insolently.

Nancy purposely avoided speaking of the marble statues at first. Instead, she tried to make the man believe she had followed him to collect damages for her car.

"So here you are," Nancy said with feigned severity. "That was a fine way to behave. Smash my bumper and then run off."

"You no talka da sense," the contractor returned excitedly. "On you I never seta da eyes before."

Nancy was astonished at the man's brazen affrontery. She determined to use a new method.

"Were you employed to haul that statue away?" she asked sternly.

"I sella da marble," the contractor explained, showing signs of becoming excited again. "He is mine."

"Yours! I am under the impression that it belongs to this estate."

"I buya da statue from what you call him—executor. And my friend, he buya from me."

Nancy turned to the other man who had stood by silently, and asked him if this were the case. The fellow declared that his friend was speaking the truth and that he himself was interested in the three statues for a cemetery. Nancy was impressed by his earnest manner, and when he gave her not only the name and location of the graveyard but his own name and address as well, she was very nearly convinced. Her half-formed resolution to notify the police weakened.

The contractor, sensing Nancy's change of attitude, was quick to try turning the situation to account. He produced a long, slender wallet from the unchartered depths of his rough wardrobe and drew forth a roll of bills.

"I make-a-da mistake," he said, a trace of fawning in

his voice. "How much-a-da cost, feex da car bumper?"

"Five dollars," Nancy answered shortly.

The man handed a five-dollar bill to Nancy.

"You have-a-da mon," he said. "Now you go—queek!"

This sudden change in the contractor's attitude was not lost upon Nancy. Her suspicions immediately were revived. She fixed indelibly in her memory the stranger's name and that of the cemetery, intending to check up on the story later.

Then, as if to confirm her new doubts, the girl noticed that every light on the truck was out. She casually mentioned the fact to the owner, who explained that the battery was low and he was trying to save it.

Nancy turned aside to look at the house. As she moved a few steps away, she heard the contractor whisper to his companion:

"Da girl, she is a snooper. We come-a back some-a other time."

The two men climbed into the truck. There was a sound of rasping gears, then the two fellows went bouncing away over the bumpy private road.

Turning sharply into the highway, the machine barely missed striking the girls' car, parked by a clump of trees. The bright headlights of the truck shot down the road in two blinding beams. The big truck roared away at high speed, conveying a piece of prized statuary to some unknown destination.

· 21 · Inside the Old House

AFTER the truck had left, Nancy went immediately to the side door of the old house. She was disappointed to find it locked.

"I'm afraid Miss Morse has left," the girl thought. "She probably returned to Sea Cliff a whole hour ago."

To make certain that no one was inside, Nancy pounded upon the panel. The sound was scarcely audible above the wild roar of the sea. The wind, too, was rising, and as the Drew girl cast a quick glance upwards at the swiftly moving clouds, she feared that the predicted storm might break at any minute.

Thinking that it would be well to test the other doors, Nancy made a tour of the mansion. She was unable to reach the rear porch for the tide was high, and angry waves were lapping over the sagging floor boards.

She stood staring up at the dark structure, thinking what a pity it was that the building now was doomed. No amount of money could save it, for it had been neglected too many years. But the furnishings might be salvaged if only someone would take the trouble.

Regretfully Nancy turned away. She had walked only a few paces when suddenly she halted. She had heard footsteps. Quietly the girl slipped behind a tall shrub.

A figure came slowly towards the house. It was Joe Mitza.

Glancing neither to right nor to left, the man walked directly to the side door. Taking a key from his pocket he fitted it into the lock.

"Where did he get that?" the girl speculated. "Miss Morse must have given it to him. But how was she able to obtain it?"

Nancy decided to secure answers to some of the questions which perplexed her. After Mitza had entered the house she did not hesitate to follow him.

After waiting for several minutes, she cautiously opened the door slightly. To her astonishment she heard the faint murmur of voices within.

"Miss Morse must be there after all!" she thought. "Either she didn't hear my knock or else she chose to ignore it."

From the sound of the voices Nancy judged that probably the couple were in the living room at the far end of the house. Cautiously she let herself into the dark hallway.

She moved noiselessly into the room to her right. As Nancy's eyes adjusted themselves to the darkness, she distinguished an elaborate marble mantel at the far end of the room. Just above it, there stood a striking model of a ship.

Nancy was certain it must be the handwrought brig of which Mr Albin had spoken, for she had never seen a more perfect piece. She ran her palm over the structure, and found it to be well preserved despite the adverse conditions to which it had been exposed.

"I must try to save it for Mr Albin," she told herself.

However, for the moment she allowed the ship to remain where it had been standing for so many years. Leaving the den, Nancy walked through another hallway, which was a passage leading to the living room.

She was now close enough to Joe Mitza and Miss Morse to realize that they were embroiled in a bitter argument. It was not a surprise to her to learn that it concerned the packet of money which Mitza had dropped in the garden.

"I thought you would take a sensible attitude about things, Miss Morse," Mitza said irritably. "I tried my best to keep our agreement. I swear I brought the money here tonight, but I dropped the roll of bills in the garden. When I went back to look for it it was gone."

"Such a story sounds very unlikely to me," Miss Morse replied tartly. "You can't expect me to turn over my five thousand dollars unless you put up a similar amount."

"I don't believe you have five thousand dollars," Mitza said crossly. "You've been stringing me along."

"Yes, I have the money," the old woman insisted. "Right here in my purse."

A little silence fell between the two, both of them hostile and calculating. Each was trying to size up the other. It seemed to Nancy as she viewed Joe Mitza's grim face in the candlelight that he was considering the possibility of taking the money forcibly from Miss Morse. The old woman appeared to divine the thought too, for instinctively she retreated a step.

The Drew girl gave the man no opportunity to carry out his evil intent. Unexpectedly, she stepped from the hall into the living room and moved into the circle of light.

Miss Morse, taken completely by surprise, cried out in alarm.

·22· *Captured*

"WHAT do you want here?" Joe Mitza demanded harshly, lifting the candlestick from the table and holding it so that the light fell full upon Nancy's face.

"You're the girl who returned my suitcase," Miss Morse stated, but there was no feeling of gratitude in her voice.

"Yes, I've been trying to see you for many days, Miss Morse."

"I can't talk with you now," the old woman interrupted impatiently. "You must go away."

"It happens that I found Mr Mitza's lost money," Nancy said quietly. She removed the roll of bills from her pocket.

Mitza reached out to snatch his property, but the girl sidestepped him.

"I want Miss Morse to see this money," she said evenly. "Look at this hundred-dollar bill closely under the light. You will be able to tell at a glance that it is counterfeit."

"Are you crazy?" Mitza demanded savagely, trying again to place himself between the girl and Miss Morse. "If the money is mine, it is genuine. How dare you hint that I would stoop to such trickery?"

Miss Morse had examined one of the bills. From her

expression, Nancy was quite certain she was convinced of its fraudulent character.

"This man meant to cheat you out of five thousand dollars," the girl explained. "He intended to take your money while he put up this worthless roll of bills. I know this to be true, for I heard him tell his scheme to a pal."

"It's not true!" Joe Mitza shouted furiously.

Miss Morse had spoken no word. For a long time she stared down at the bill in her hand. Unquestionably, the revelation had stunned her. Nancy expected to receive at least a measure of gratitude, and so was dumb-founded when the old woman, without the slightest warning whirled round to face her.

"I don't believe a word of your brazen lies," she snapped. "You made up every bit of it."

"Sure she did," Mitza sang out triumphantly.

"But I can prove—" Nancy began.

The woman would not allow her to finish. "This is my affair and you're not to interfere," she said harshly. "I told you on the train that I could look after myself. Now get out of here and don't come back! You had no business to trespass in the first place."

"Had you?" the girl countered, but Miss Morse made no answer.

All the fervour seemed to have left the old woman, and she sat down wearily in one of the dusty chairs. The flickering candlelight revealed that her face was distorted with various emotions.

Suddenly, without knowing why, Nancy felt sorry for the aged woman. She appeared very miserable and unhappy, yet was determined to accept no help in her affairs.

"Very well, Miss Morse, I'll go," Nancy said quietly.

"I'm sorry to have caused you so much trouble for I only wished to be of help."

She waited a moment, half expecting that the woman would reply, but Miss Morse averted her glance and remained silent.

Nancy walked slowly from the room. When she reached the hall, she heard a shrill whistle come from somewhere in the grounds.

"A police signal!" the girl thought.

Before she could make a single movement, Joe Mitza blew out the candle, plunging the living room into darkness.

Nancy felt herself grasped rudely from behind. Miss Morse's bony hand was clapped over her mouth. As she struggled to free herself, she was amazed to discover that the woman was strong as a man.

The girl, taken unaware, was no match for Miss Morse, yet she might have broken away had not Mitza come to the assistance of the woman. The pair worked silently, but with a skill as amazing as it was disconcerting.

Nancy found herself bound and gagged in the twinkling of an eye. She was shoved into a closet and the door slammed shut.

"Hide," Miss Morse ordered tersely. "They're coming in to look for us."

Nancy could not understand why the old woman should be afraid of the police, for until this moment she had never suspected that Miss Morse might be a fugitive from justice.

"I should have been warned when I found that suitcase with the wig in it," she thought belatedly.

Nancy heard Miss Morse and Mitza scurrying about

the room in their search for a safe hiding place. Then the mansion became quiet, but only for a minute. Suddenly there came a loud pounding on the side door.

"Open up!" a voice commanded.

The order was repeated, and finally Nancy heard the police officers come tramping through the hallway. A moment more, and she knew they must have reached the living room. She struggled and twisted in an effort to make some sound which would draw attention to her.

"I guess it was only a false alarm," she heard one of the local officers say gruffly. "That old man didn't know what he was talking about when he said a woman was trying to steal things from the homestead. No one has been here for years."

It occurred to Nancy that probably the men had been sent to the Conger estate by Mr Albin, who might have recovered from his heart attack sufficiently to talk to the officials by telephone. Again she tried to attract attention, but the slight sounds she made were nullified by the howling of the wind, the roar of the sea, and the voices of the investigators.

"We'll take a routine look upstairs," one of the men said. "But the place is deserted."

Nancy heard the officers tramping over the floor above her, then she followed their progress as they returned downstairs.

"Let's go, fellows," one of the men urged. "A bad storm is brewing and we want to get back to town before it breaks."

"Listen to this old house creak and groan," another muttered uneasily. "It's fairly straining to fall into the sea."

Nancy listened with sinking heart to the sound of

receding footsteps. A door slammed. Then the place became quiet once more.

Soon the girl heard a slight movement in the room. She sensed that Miss Morse was emerging from her hiding place. Apparently she was joined by Joe Mitza, for the man said with an attempt at nonchalance:

"Well, they've gone. Not that I was afraid to be found here, but it's always just as well not to invite an investigation. Police like to dig up false facts and put blame upon anyone they can."

"I understand—perfectly," Miss Morse replied, and there was bitterness in her voice.

The pair made no reference in their conversation to Nancy, and the girl began to wonder if they had forgotten about her. The closet was dusty and close. She felt half suffocated.

"I believe they mean to leave me here," she thought in terror. "Unless I can get out by my own efforts, my only hope of rescue lies with George and Bess."

Nancy knew only too well that her chums would not venture near the house until a considerable length of time had elapsed. She must depend upon her own ingenuity if she were to escape.

"The old mansion may wash into the sea at any moment, too," she told herself fearfully.

Spurred by that unpleasant prospect, Nancy began to work frantically at her bonds.

Draped in White

FOR some minutes, Nancy was too occupied with her own particular set of troubles to pay much attention to the loud, excited conversation of Mitza and Miss Morse. As she squirmed this way and that, trying to loosen her hands, she gathered that Mitza was trying to reinstate himself in the old woman's graces. Failing in that, he began to threaten her.

"You can't pull the wool over my eyes," he said harshly. "Let's end the pretence. After the way you acted when the police were here, I know you're not as innocent as you've pretended. You probably have a record."

Nancy was unable to catch Miss Morse's reply. She lost the conversation entirely, as she worked at the cords which bound her hands. They loosened a trifle, and she grew hopeful that soon she would succeed in freeing herself.

Then one of Miss Morse's remarks caught Nancy's attention. It was of such startling significance that she listened intently.

"Very well, Mitza," the old woman said tremulously, "I am tired of your nagging. I'll tell you the unpleasant truth, which you have brought upon yourself."

"What do you mean?" the man demanded.

"Just this. I've known that you thought me an innocent dupe, but I had reasons of my own for pretending that I didn't."

"What's your game?" Mitza asked sharply.

"I have no game. I am an old woman now, and life doesn't hold much for me any more."

"I don't see what you are trying to tell me. I doubt if you know yourself."

"My real name is not Miss Morse," she went on patiently, "nor is yours Mitza."

"You're wrong there. My name is Mitza."

"No," the woman denied, "you just think it is. If you will listen instead of interrupting, I'll try to tell you everything."

"Who are you?" Mitza persisted.

"My name is Bernice Conger. I am the daughter of the former owner of this house. Once I lived here happily, and had everything a girl could ask for, but I ran away from home when I was eighteen years old. I eloped with a worthless man who turned out to be a crook."

"What is that to me?" Mitza demanded.

"Wait, I am coming to that. My husband was always in trouble with the law, but as I loved him and didn't want to give him up, I worked with him. We completed several deals together, so that in the end I was involved as deeply as he was. We smuggled goods across the Canadian border and defrauded several individuals."

"That was hazardous," Mitza said sneeringly. "I'll bet they sent you up for that."

"Yes," the old woman answered wearily. "My husband served ten years in prison. I received a lighter sentence."

"I don't see what this has to do with me."

"You are my son!"

"Your son?" Mitza gasped in shock.

"So it startles you? I was astonished too, when I first saw you on the train, but the resemblance to your father is marked."

"You must be mistaken," Mitza muttered slowly. "I couldn't be your son."

"I am not mistaken. I placed you in an institution when you were seven years of age. I sent money regularly for your care, but I never went to see you."

"What was the name of the place?" Mitza asked.

"The Elmwood Home for Children."

Miss Morse's answer left the man somewhat shaken, for he knew well enough that his early years had been spent in that institution. When but sixteen years of age he had run away, managing for himself and learning to get on in the world by his own resourcefulness.

"I always hoped that you would grow up to be a fine man and go straight," the old woman continued in a voice tense with emotion. "I ruined my own life. I wanted you to make something of yours. I didn't want you ever to know that your parents had been in prison.

"I had no intention of revealing myself to you. Then when I heard your voice on the train I knew you were my son. I encouraged you to become friendly, wanting to meet you again."

"So you tricked me——"

"I shouldn't call it that. You were my son, and even if I have made a horrible botch of my own life, I have feelings the same as other mothers. I can't tell you what a blow it was to me when I discovered that like your father, you loved easy money."

"Where is my father?" Mitza asked harshly.

"I don't know. I haven't seen him in years. Sometimes I think he is dead."

As the talk went on, Nancy learned more of the strange, depressing life which Miss Morse had led. Since leaving prison, the woman had been hounded by the police so that many times, in order to escape questioning, she had been compelled to resort to some sort of a disguise. She was skilled in the use of make-up, so it was not difficult for her to pass as a woman in her thirties. The loss of her suitcase containing the costume and wig had frightened her until it had been returned by Nancy Drew.

Joe Mitza had received a rude shock when he learned the identity of the woman he had attempted to cheat. The story depressed him, yet he could not doubt its truth. If he felt the slightest feeling of affection for the pathetic old creature he did not disclose it by his words.

Nancy had heard enough of the conversation to comprehend a great many things which previously had mystified her. She understood now why Miss Morse had resented the girl's attempts to expose Mitza. And the woman's presence in the old house no longer was baffling. The property actually belonged to her, and doubtless she had kept a key since that day many years before when she had left home.

Nancy's fingers were not idle as she listened to the amazing tale. Presently she had freed one arm. Then it became easy for her to loosen her other bonds. Next she jerked off the gag.

Pushing the door open a tiny crack, Nancy peered into the living room. Mitza and his mother were at the opposite end, their backs towards the closet. They were talking so earnestly that they did not hear the girl.

Nancy thought that possibly she might reach the corridor without being seen. She stole noiselessly from the closet, halting in panic as a board creaked.

Neither Mitza nor Miss Morse seemed aware of Nancy. As the woman wept, her son berated her for being such a sentimental fool.

Nancy felt sorry for Miss Morse, but having learned the truth, she knew there was no way she could help the woman. Mitza and his mother must solve their own problems. For the moment, her sole thought was to escape from the house.

The girl's hand touched the corner of a dusty sheet which covered one of the chairs. Impulsively she wrapped it about her, and like a ghost glided silently across to the hall.

Reaching the open air, Nancy caught her breath in surprise. Since she had entered the house, the wind had risen steadily. It whipped the sheet and almost tore it from her grasp. The sea was running high, and she could hear great waves pounding against the sand bank on which the old house rested.

Nancy was tempted to hasten back to the car where she knew Bess and George would be awaiting her anxiously. However, she did not wish to leave until after Mitza had gone.

"He should be coming out soon," she thought, glancing speculatively at the clouds overhead.

She wondered how much longer the storm would hold off. The tall trees near the place were waving wildly in the wind, and at any moment a limb might snap off and come crashing down. The site was a most dangerous one.

Nancy stood hesitating for an instant; then, with the wind tearing at her garments, she crossed the garden towards the Whispering Girl statue. Where three figures previously had stood, only two now remained.

"What a pity to ruin the group," the girl thought. Then she heard a door slam shut.

"It's Mitza!" she told herself.

Nancy scarcely had time to hide. Wrapping the sheet tightly about her, she stepped up to the empty pedestal to become a living statue in the Whispering Girl group.

·24·   *The Storm*

WITH head bent low, Joe Mitza stumbled through the garden. He was muttering to himself that he had learned his lesson, and that never again would he be dishonest. The fellow glanced at the Whispering Girl statue, then hastened down the road.

"And now to find George and Bess," Nancy told herself. "If we hurry we can still get back to Sea Cliff before the storm breaks."

The sheet offered some protection from the wild wind, so she kept it wrapped about her as she hastened to the main road.

"The girls will think they're seeing a ghost when I walk into view," she chuckled.

An instant later the smile had left Nancy's face. Mr Trixler's car had disappeared!

She remembered the exact place where the girls had parked and found where the car wheels had stood, but there was no sign of her chums.

"They've left me!" she acknowledged ruefully. "Now I am in a predicament, stranded in this desolate place with a storm coming on."

Nancy did not believe that her chums had really deserted her. She thought they might have become alarmed over her prolonged absence and gone back to Sea Cliff for help. The result, however, was the same.

"Well, I'm not alone here anyway," she thought, turning to retrace her steps to the Conger house. "Miss Morse is still inside that old dwelling. I ought to warn her to leave, for the place might collapse."

It was not necessary for Nancy to enter the house. When she reached the garden she was relieved to see Miss Morse emerging from the side door wearing no hat or coat, and her hair blowing wildly in the wind.

Miss Morse stood still for a moment and leaned against the crumbling wall of the house. Then she stumbled towards the black, angry waters of the encroaching sea.

Fearing that the distraught woman intended to fling herself over the bank, Nancy made a move to start after her. Miss Morse suddenly turned and came aimlessly towards the garden.

The Drew girl did not wish to be seen. With the sheet wrapped about her she once more assumed the pose of a statue, remaining motionless as the woman staggered towards her. Miss Morse dropped down upon one knee. With her head bent low she began to pray, asking forgiveness for the wicked life which she had led.

At first Nancy kept silent, scarcely daring to move a muscle lest she be discovered. Then she whispered a few consoling words in an attempt to calm Miss Morse.

Slowly the old lady raised her head, as if to hear more clearly. Her lips moved, yet she spoke no word. Confident that Miss Morse believed the statue had spoken, Nancy offered additional spiritual advice.

Suddenly, the girl received a shock that nearly caused her to abandon her pose as a marble figure. The woman, assuming the message had come from her dead husband, spoke to him. To Nancy's amazement, she addressed him as Frank Wormrath. He must be the dishonest partner of her father's client, Mr Owen!

"Your husband is not dead," the girl whispered when she had recovered her poise again. "Do not fear. He still lives."

A flash of lightning cut a jagged ribbon through the inky sky, momentarily illuminating the garden. Rain began to fall. Miss Morse was not aware of the storm, for she still knelt, waiting for the statue to speak again.

"Seek shelter within the house," Nancy directed in a whisper, for she was eager to leave herself. Her sheet was becoming water soaked, and soon the deception would be revealed.

Miss Morse moved silently away towards the building. As soon as she dared, Nancy followed. She knew that with the high waves pounding against the foundation of the structure it would be unsafe to remain there long. Yet they could not stay out in the drenching rain.

"As soon as the storm lets up a bit I'll find a safer place for both of us," she told herself.

Nancy quietly entered the house, and tossed away her wet sheet. She scarcely knew how to approach the old woman.

"Miss Morse! Miss Morse!" she called softly.

There was no response. Suddenly she heard a low

moan coming from the floor. Groping her way forward, she found the candle which Mitza had left on the table, and beside it a box of matches.

In a moment she made a light, which revealed Miss Morse lying in a crumpled heap on the floor. The woman had fainted. Nancy ran to her, pillowing the inert head upon her lap.

"Poor thing," she thought, "she has had too much excitement. No wonder she collapsed."

The girl was alarmed upon taking Miss Morse's pulse to discover that it was rapid and weak. However, in a few minutes the old woman's eyes opened feebly and she stared blankly into the girl's face.

"Who—are—you?" she whispered.

"A friend," Nancy answered soothingly. "Don't try to talk. Just as soon as the rain stops I shall take you to a doctor."

The storm, however, showed no signs of abating. Each time the high waves struck the decaying foundation of the house, Nancy could hear the rotted timbers shudder and groan. Outside, the rain fell in torrents. Wind rattled the windows.

Miss Morse seemed to have fallen into a state of semi-stupor. She was fully conscious, yet appeared hardly aware of anything going on about her. She clung tightly to Nancy's hand.

Presently the girl went over to the window to gaze out at the tempest. She wondered what had become of George and Bess.

As she walked back across the floor to Miss Morse's side there came a resounding crack and roar as a gigantic wave struck the foundation of the mansion. It was far worse than any previous blow had been. Nancy was thrown off balance, and the old woman suddenly seemed to comprehend their danger.

"Help! Help!" the old woman screamed in terror as she too, pitched forward. "The house is falling!"

The ancient dwelling shivered and groaned as if struggling to hold its precarious balance on the sandy bank. The furniture danced crazily on the floor. Everywhere bric-a-brac fell.

Slowly at first, then with a sickening plunge, the great homestead with its two helpless occupants toppled over the bank to be claimed by the triumphant sea!

·25·   *Adrift*

LEFT alone in the automobile by the highway, Bess and George had waited patiently for the return of their chum. They were startled into alertness as a truck came careening down the private road directly towards them.

Before either of the girls could shout a warning, the contractor who was at the wheel had swerved his machine just enough to miss the car. George and Bess were unable to recognize him in the dark.

"I wonder what that man was doing at Old Estate?" Bess speculated, staring after the disappearing vehicle.

"Nancy will know the answer, you may be sure," George chuckled. "Just wait until she gets back. If I had her nerve I'd have gone along and helped to investigate."

"Nancy has the heart of a lion," Bess replied, "but I can't help feeling she's too venturesome—especially tonight."

"I wish she would hurry. If she doesn't, we'll be caught in the storm."

Half an hour elapsed, and still Nancy did not appear.

"Let's go after her," George proposed suddenly. "I'm beginning to think something has happened."

Bess did not favour the idea, but she too was worried about her chum. After some discussion, they drove the car up the bumpy road. The old mansion appeared to be completely deserted, and Nancy was nowhere about.

The girls called their chum's name several times. They did not believe she had gone inside the house, for they remembered that the doors and windows of the ancient dwelling had been locked.

"Whatever became of her?" Bess gasped, now thoroughly frightened. "Was she in that truck?"

For the first time it dawned upon the girls that Nancy might have been kidnapped. The thought became a conviction.

"We must go for help," George cried. "Mr Drew will know just what to do."

To drive the entire way back to Sea Cliff would consume considerable time, but the girls remembered a store not more than a mile away where they could telephone. Soon they had Carson Drew on the wire and were pouring out their story to him. The lawyer, greatly worried over Nancy's disappearance, instructed them to remain where they were. He would join them by taxi.

Mr Drew, telling the driver this was an emergency, asked the man to make all possible speed. It was raining by the time he reached the store where George and Bess were waiting. Unmindful of the storm, the three set off in Mr Trixler's car for Old Estate. On their way there, the girls told him exactly what had happened to them since they had left the hotel earlier in the day.

As the car halted at the main road, George cast a startled glance at her two companions. She had heard a strange reverberating crash come from the direction of Old Estate.

"What was that?" she asked. "It sounded just as if the house had tumbled into the sea!"

By this time the private road was too muddy for a car to travel over. Abandoning the automobile, the three ran towards the house. The rain fell in such torrents that they were unable to distinguish anything until they were very close to the place.

"Why, the house is gone!" Bess cried, ending in a little scream. "It's floating away into the sea!"

The three rushed on to the bank. Through the rain they were able to make out a large, dark object some distance from shore.

"Nancy couldn't be in there!" George gasped in horror.

Carson Drew cupped his hands and shouted:

"Ahoy! Ahoy out there!"

They heard no answering cry. But then it was improbable that the sound of his voice would carry.

"I'm sure Nancy couldn't be aboard," Mr Drew said, though his tone lacked conviction.

"The house won't stay afloat long, will it?" Bess asked in a hushed tone.

"Not in this sea," the lawyer answered grimly. "It's probably slowly filling with water. If anyone is aboard——"

"Isn't there something we can do to make certain?" George questioned anxiously.

"Yes, there is," Carson Drew answered shortly.

"We'll bring the Coast Guards."

The lawyer sent the girls by car to the nearest telephone, while he remained at Old Estate trying to keep watch of the floating house. Unmindful of the drenching rain, he maintained a faithful vigil. Presently, despite his best efforts, the dark hulk vanished into the darkness.

"I know Nancy couldn't be out there," he whispered to himself, "yet something keeps telling me she is. Oh, why don't those Coast Guards get here?"

Bess and George hurried over to the telephone. While it seemed that considerable time had elapsed, actually the Coast Guard crew arrived upon the scene in a very short time. The men were well equipped for any emergency, and with powerful searchlights, sought to locate the floating house.

Soon the giant beam focused upon it and the watchers on shore saw that it was low in the water.

"Can't you find out if anyone is aboard?" the lawyer asked. "Launch a boat and——"

"Not in this sea," the other responded with a shake of his head. "It wouldn't last a minute in those waves."

"There is someone in the house!" George suddenly cried, gripping the man's hand, and pointing towards an upper window of the abode. "It looks like Nancy!"

"It *is* Nancy!" Carson Drew exclaimed in horror. "She's trying to signal with a candle, but the light is so dim one scarcely can see it."

"Oh, will they be able to save her, do you think?" Bess moaned, clinging tightly to George's hand. "The house is moving away so rapidly, and I heard one of the men say it couldn't last another fifteen minutes."

"They expect to bring Nancy in by means of a

breeches-buoy," George answered soberly. "But if the line should miss the house, or if Nancy should be unable to connect it——"

She broke off and could not finish. It seemed an eternity before the Coast Guard line finally whizzed through the air.

"Straight through a window!" one of the men exclaimed in satisfaction. "A bull's-eye!"

The line was pulled taut, and those on shore knew that Nancy had obeyed the instructions which had been sent with the rocket. Everyone drew a sigh of relief as the contrivance was drawn into the mansion.

"Nancy will be safe in just a moment more," George said consolingly to Mr Drew.

Presently, through the rain, the watchers saw the breeches-buoy coming slowly towards them with a dark figure clinging to the supports.

"Why, it's not Nancy at all!" Bess exclaimed. "It's Miss Morse!"

As the old woman was lifted out, she gasped that the Drew girl was still aboard the floating house.

"She made me go first," Miss Morse murmured. "The place is filling up with water—it won't last long. Save her!" The bedraggled figure collapsed in the arms of a Coast Guard man and was carried away.

The breeches-buoy made its slow trip back to the derelict building. There was a delay, and then it started on the return journey.

"It's Nancy!" George cried in relief. "And she's carrying something in her arms. Can it be a child?"

As the rescue apparatus came closer, Bess and George were inclined to chuckle, for the "child" was the cumbersome ship model which Mr Albin coveted so much. Nancy had remembered how the old gentleman had craved for the trophy, and had saved it for him.

"How thankful I am that you are safe," said Mr Drew as he helped to lift out his daughter and enfold her, ship and all, in his arms.

"The house is breaking up!" one of the Coast Guard men cried.

Everyone peered out across the angry waters where he was playing the beam of light. The building seemed to crumble. One portion sank beneath the surface while the other floated away, no longer in an upright position.

"You didn't get out of there one second too soon, Nancy," Mr Drew shuddered.

"I owe my life to you all," the girl replied soberly. "We were drifting to sea so fast I didn't expect to be rescued. How did you know I was inside the house?"

Carson Drew explained that George and Bess had brought him to the scene. Nancy then thanked her chums, but they cut short the little speech by insisting that she hurry back to the hotel for warm clothing and a hot drink.

At Sea Cliff again, and feeling none the worse for her adventure, Nancy had a strange tale to relate. Carson Drew was amazed to learn of Miss Morse's relationship not only to Mitza, but also to Frank Wormrath, his client's partner.

The following day Nancy visited Miss Morse at the hospital. She was sorry to learn that the old woman had contracted a severe cold as the result of her night of exposure, and was in a generally weakened condition. The girl was permitted to talk with the patient for only a few minutes.

"I shall die," the old woman whispered as Nancy

moved close to hear her words. "But I do not care. I am old and my life is ruined. If only I might see my son again and know that he will mend his evil ways, I shall die happier."

"I am sure he will go straight," Nancy assured her. "As he stumbled from the house last night, I heard him mumble that he never intends to do wrong again."

Miss Morse seemed to be comforted by this infor- but two days later, she lapsed into a coma from which she never aroused.

It was a relief to the Drew girl and her friends to observe that Mr Owen improved in health steadily. One afternoon, when the nurse had been dismissed, they joined Mrs Owen in her husband's room, and the couple learned for the first time the entire history of Miss Morse's strange life.

"Dad has checked up on the information," Nancy ended her story. "The woman's husband is without question the same Frank Wormrath who tricked you, Mr Owen. The fellow is fearful that his prison record will be exposed, so he has agreed to settle with you at your own terms."

"Did you say that Miss Morse's true name was Bernice Conger?" Mrs Owen asked in astonishment.

"Yes, she was Mr Conger's long-lost daughter."

"I have never told you this, Nancy, but I knew Bernice when she was a girl," Mrs Owen said slowly. "I spent a summer here in Sea Cliff with my parents. We often played together at the Conger estate. I saw the Whispering Girl statue for the first time then. Later I came back here to view it again."

"And you haven't seen Miss Morse in recent years?" Nancy inquired.

"No, and it is a great shock to me to learn of her end. She used to write me letters occasionally." Mrs Owen hesitated, then said with a change of tone, "Why, it was Bernice who led me to believe that my husband meant to desert me when he went to Borneo!"

"What reason would she have had for doing such a thing?" Nancy asked in amazement.

"I think I know why she tried to separate us," Mr Owen interrupted. "I had forgotten until now, but when I was in New York ready to sail, Bernice Conger learned that I was there. She came to see me to borrow money. I was unable to grant her wish for she asked for a very large sum."

"You think the woman sought revenge?" Nancy questioned.

"Yes, I'm sure of it," Mr Owen answered. "Come to think of it, the information that my wife was dead, easily could have been sent by her."

"I don't see how Bernice had the heart to be so cruel as to try to separate us," Mrs Owen murmured. "The only explanation is that trouble twisted her mind."

"Let's be thankful that all our years were not wasted," Mr Owen smiled, squeezing his wife's hand. "How much we owe to Nancy Drew and her father."

"Yes, we'll never be able to repay them," agreed the clubwoman. "I tried for years to trace you, Charles, inserting advertisements in various newspapers. They were all in vain until Nancy chanced to see one of the items."

Mr Drew had learned from his daughter that to all appearances the contractor had stolen one of the smaller marble figures from the Conger Estate. He immediately began an investigation which exposed the theft, and compelled the fellow and his friend to return the statue.

Nancy worried about the Whispering Girl group, feeling certain it would be ruined if allowed to remain at the deserted Conger Estate. She was elated when her father brought word that the management of the Seaside Hotel had purchased the three statues, intending to reset them on their own beautiful grounds.

"I'm very glad," Nancy declared, "for now those lovely pieces will be preserved for years to come."

Before Nancy and her friends left Sea Cliff, the marble group was transferred to its new location. A special, though rather informal, dedication ceremony was held in connection with the unveiling. Nancy played an important rôle and was introduced to the audience as the Whispering Girl in person. She was made up especially for the occasion, and as she posed beside the statue, everyone found the resemblance startling.

The final event of the programme was a surprise even to Nancy. Town officials presented her with a little bronze medal for her bravery in saving poor Bernice Conger from drowning.

"Well, I guess all the excitement is over," Bess sighed blissfully at the end of the day. "It's too bad Nancy can't think of another mystery to solve."

Of course the Drew girl never planned such things. Puzzles to solve just came her way, as they did in her next adventure, *The Haunted Showboat*.

"I know one that's still as baffling as ever," George chuckled.

"What is that?" Nancy inquired innocently.

"The mystery of Togo's ownership."

"He isn't worrying about it, so neither shall I," his new mistress laughed, as she stooped to pick up the little dog. "From now on, Togo belongs to me."